LISTEN FOR THE CRICKETS

LISTEN FOR THE CRICKETS

CHAD GUNTER

Acrasia Media

Contents

1   The Con Man   1

2   The Prostitute   3

3   The Preacher   7

4   The Tomboy   10

5   The Psychopath   13

6   The Actress   18

7   The Kid   22

8   The Settling   27

9   Collection Agency   32

10 Shock   47

11 Transmission Received   49

12 Interception   56

13 Missouri Loves Company   64

14 Pursuits   71

15 Never Too Late to Change   74

16 Guess Who's Coming for Sinners?   82

17 Good Thing, Small Package 84

18 The New Leader 91

19 The Discovery 96

20 It's Not What You Got 99

21 A Little R & R 105

22 New Set of Wheels 112

23 Kaletta 116

24 On the Road Again 118

25 Into the Fire? 122

26 Free Ride 128

27 The Complex 130

28 Heard 'Round the World 146

29 "Nick" of Time 148

Epilogue 153
Author's Note 155
Other Books by the Author 157

LISTEN FOR THE CRICKETS
Published by Acrasia Media
Charlotte, North Carolina

This book is a work of fiction. The characters and events portrayed in this book are fictitious, although the locations are real. Any similarities to real persons, living or dead, are coincidental, and not intended by the author.

Copyright © 2022 by Chad Eric Gunter

Publisher's Cataloging-in-Publication data

Names: Gunter, Chad Eric, author.
Title: Listen for the crickets / Chad Eric Gunter.
Description: Charlotte, NC: Acrasia Media, 2022.
Identifiers: ISBN: 978-1-958202-05-0 (hardback) | 978-1-958202-11-1 (paperback) | 978-1-958202-08-1 (ePub)
Subjects: LCSH Human-alien encounters--Fiction. | End of the world--Fiction. | Science fiction. | Adventure fiction. | BISAC FICTION / Science Fiction / General | FICTION / Science Fiction / Action & Adventure | FICTION / Science Fiction / Alien Contact | FICTION / Science Fiction / Apocalyptic & Post-Apocalyptic
Classification: LCC PS3607 .U4815 L57 2022 | DDC 813.6--dc23

Second Printing, 2022

I

The Con Man

"Ah, come on, Ted. It's a golden opportunity! You can double your money!" said the con man. "If it's such a great deal, then why are you offering it to me?" asked Ted sharply. Ted was no fool. "Look at this gold watch. Look at this Italian suit. Do I look like I really need the money? I just figured I'd pass on some of the wealth." said Marty Maxx, the con man, as he showed off his "expensive" habiliments. "Since when do you do favors for anyone?" asked Ted sarcastically. Marty started to snap back a reply, but Ted flickered as if he was a staticky TV station struggling to form a picture and then vanished. Marty's jaw dropped. A few cars parked along the curb of Main Street began to flicker and disappear. A taxi went by in front of him. The rear of the taxi flickered and then was gone. The remaining front half of the taxi dropped with a clang to make contact with the street. It slid for several hundred feet, as sparks shot out from under it before it came to a halt. The New York City taxi driver looked back, stunned. He no longer had a passenger. Marty whirled around and began maneuvering his way through the crowded sidewalk. Everyone was in a panic, and some people were screaming and running as they began to witness the chaos. Marty headed toward what he hoped to be his solace. He had made many successful deals in Pete's Café. It was like his hunting ground. He felt at home there. He paused at the door to the café and glanced back before he went in. He heard explosions erupting off in the distance. He saw some buildings collapsing. As he turned to go in, an elderly woman was coming out. He shoved her aside. When the door closed behind him, it disappeared. He was the only one inside the café who wanted to remain in it. Everyone else was running out. That suited him fine. He went as far into the back of the café as he could. He found a storage room, went in, and closed the door behind him. He sat down in the dark. He pushed as far back up against the wall as he could go, and waited for whatever was going to happen.

2

The Prostitute

Mandy was in the shower scrubbing herself from head to toe. She reprimanded herself as always for doing what she does for a living. Her clientele consisted of a few well-to-do men who were all married and used her to put a little excitement in their lives. The men she shared herself with were "regulars" that usually made dates every other month or so. Their extreme generosity for her services meant that she not only did not have to meet the men frequently but also gave her the opportunity to pursue an education. She hoped to quickly have the tools to obtain a lucrative and legitimate career. Although Mandy was very intelligent, her lack of formal education would mean that she would have to essentially work forever in this small town, and the timetable to better herself was simply un-realistic. The circumstances that had brought her to this town, and basically off of the radar, were through no fault of her own. She by no means condoned her own actions in the matter but felt she was doing the best she could with the resources she had in order to meet the goals she had made.

At the beginning of each of her "relationships," each of the three men had been concerned and questioned her about the AIDS virus and other health concerns. That gave her a little comfort with the fact that they probably didn't have any STDs, and didn't want to get one any more than she did. Safe sex was always practiced, and so far, there were no accidents. Most people in Zebulon, Georgia were clean and decent anyway. It was a very small, country town, with very few newcomers. Mandy had been one of the newcomers. But she was walking a tightrope, and she knew it.

Mandy was absorbed in her thoughts of a better life when there was a loud explosion, and her apartment building shook. She hurriedly stepped out of the shower and draped a towel around herself. She went to the window and looked out. Her eyes widened. A building larger than the one she was in, and less than three blocks away, had crumbled and was in flames. As she stared, shocked at the site, there was another explosion. She felt her building move. She heard screams throughout the apartment building. The sound of people running echoed from the hallways. Someone was going from door to door, knocking and yelling for everyone to get out of the building. When the knocking and yelling came to her door, it snapped her out of her daze. She headed to the door but paused when she realized she was wearing only a towel. She quickly grabbed some things from her dresser. She glanced around briefly, and then picked up her pocketbook. She slipped on a robe, and clutched her clothes and pocketbook tightly, then hurried out the door.

Panic was in the air. People were pushing and shoving, trying to get to the stairs. Groups of people moved as one. Gradually, she made it into a steady stream of people, heading down the stairs. After four stories of traveling, she was whisked out of the building along with the crowd. People were dispersing in all directions. Mandy looked up at the sky to see some streaks of light passing by. There were more explosions. Some were very far away, but some were close enough to make the ground shake. She looked at the building she had just come from. There was a large, gaping hole in the side, big enough to drive a truck through. There was another large explosion nearby. Particles of building materials rained down all around. Mandy Richards was on the verge of panicking when she suddenly had a flashback of her first appearance in court when she had first been arrested for prostitution. That was the most embarrassing day of her life. She was fined fifty dollars and time served, for the few days, she had spent in jail. She had since learned many things. The moment she now remembered was when she was leaving the courthouse. There was a small sign on the wall that read "BOMB SHELTER" in bold letters. She began running the four blocks to the courthouse. Her bare feet slapped the sidewalk. Her robe flapped in the wind, offering brief glimpses of her nakedness. Any other day, heads would have been turning, to see the attractive, slender 27-year-old woman with long black hair. But today, people were terrified. The only thing they were looking for was shelter from the fast-approaching terror.

She relaxed her grip on her clothes and purse as she slowed down in front of the courthouse. There were several buildings on fire, and a few were completely destroyed. There were some bloody bodies lying in the street and on the sidewalks. People were yelling, screaming, and running in all directions as if they were crazy. *Maybe they were.* Mandy thought. She held onto her own sanity as she sprinted up the courthouse stairs. As she approached the door, she found an old man lying on his side, holding his hand to his head. There was a little blood on him. She stooped down beside him to help. He weakly said, "They pushed me down, runnin' from the courthouse." She looked at his wound. On the surface, it didn't seem too bad, but she didn't really know how hard his head hat been hit, either. "Hold tightly to my hand. Let's get you up and into the courthouse. We'll be safer there," Mandy said as she helped the man up. "Yes Ma'am, thank you." he said. Mandy smiled at the man as they went through the door, leaning on each other.

There was no one in the courthouse. The safest place in town, and no one was there but Mandy and the old man. "I guess it's just you and me." she said. "The basement's that way." said the old man pointing down the hallway. Mandy helped the old man along as he led them to the basement. They had to make the last flight of stairs in the dark. When they reached the bottom, she helped the old man down, so he could sit on the bottom step. She looked through her pocketbook. She had a pack of matches that she had picked up from a Chinese restaurant. She lit one of them, and looked around the room. For the brief 20 seconds that the match burned, she saw some old desks, file cabinets, chairs, and other outdated, dusty office equipment. None of the chairs looked as comfortable as the bottom step did. When the match went out, she took advantage of the darkness to slip into her clothes. She was relieved that she had picked up a pair of jeans. After she was dressed, she lit another match, and let the old man hold it. She ripped part of her robe, and wiped the dirt from his head. He flinched. "I'm sorry." she said softly. "That's okay," he said. Mandy wrapped a strip of the robe around his head like a bandanna, to protect the wound. "Thank you, pretty lady." he said. "You're welcome." Mandy said. She sat down beside the old man and cupped one of his hands into both of hers.

3

The Preacher

"*...Fear not; I am the first and the last: I am he that liveth, and was dead; and, behold, I am alive forevermore, Amen; and have the keys of hell and of death,*" quoted the preacher from Revelation 1:17-18. There was a rumbling off in the distance. "My lost souls, we are all sinners. We are all unworthy of the glory of God." said the preacher. He slowly bowed his head. He had a death grip on the pulpit. His knuckles had turned white. Preacher John Briggs was a very tall man. His dark hair was slick and combed back. He always had an unfriendly look on his face unless you were coming into his church before a sermon, or leaving it after one. The folks of this community didn't like their new preacher. He had been there for six months now. They thought that maybe they would grow to like him. The only thing that was growing was the number of empty pews each Sunday. Some people on the outskirts of Shreveport, Louisiana, were taking the long drive to town for their Sunday worship. Some people had just disappeared.

There were some loud, sonic booms outside of the church,

followed by smaller explosions. Many people in the church gasped, and several stood up. Preacher Briggs' head snapped up. "People!" he yelled. "Quiet! The Almighty won't appreciate any disrespect!" The men and women that had stood up, sat back down. There was still some whispering, and looking around. There were many different sounds of rumbling and explosions spaced several seconds apart. The small church shook. A ten-foot square section of the roof of the church disappeared. Some of the congregation began to moan with fear. Many people stood up to ready themselves to run. Preacher Briggs ran from the pulpit down the aisle, and yelled for the people to control themselves and sit back down. As if young children, scolded by a parent, they did so. "You must realize that if He wants you, He will get you! No matter where you go, or what you do!" Preacher Briggs began yelling to his flock as he continued down the aisle, walking backwards with his arms out-stretched as he preached. He reached the door. "I say we open our hearts to God!" he said as he swung the old door open. The congregation watched him walk outside and pull the door closed behind him. They waited for the door to reopen.

They waited thirty seconds.

They waited a minute.

They waited a minute and a half.

The church continued shaking. The explosions continued booming. One man jumped up from his pew and ran to the door to look out. "Oh my God! It's locked! The preacher has locked us inside!" he yelled. There was a singular movement as everyone quickly stood from the pews, and began running around in the church trying to find a way out. The door at the other end was also locked. An elderly woman was banging her bible up against a stained-glass window. Her husband came up beside her holding a folding chair. He motioned her aside and then smashed the chair against the window. Some of the panels broke, but the window was old, with a good, solid frame. The flimsy folding chair was no match for it. Everyone was gathered at the broken window, furiously trying to break more open. Through the broken glass panels, they saw flames and destruction off in the distance. Some people fell to the floor, crying.

The preacher sifted through his keys after he locked the door. He sprinted to his old, beat-up pickup truck. The door squeaked when he opened it. He had to slam it hard to shut it. It was old and rusty, but the engine roared to life on the first try. "Nice day for a Sunday drive." Preacher Briggs said to himself. He drove once around the church before he headed down the dirt road. The Preacher had it in his mind to head in the direction of Shreveport. After all, that's probably where a lot of those sinners that used to come to his church on Sundays were. Maybe he'd stop by, and see how they were doing.

As the people struggled to get the windows broken open far enough to get through, they saw Preacher Briggs' old pickup truck circle around in front of them. He was just close enough to them so they could see him looking back at them, with a big smile on his face. They all looked momentarily quietened down and looked at each other in shock. As the old truck disappeared from view, the entire church, along with all of the people inside, flickered, and then was gone. What a day the preacher had chosen to finally flip out.

4

The Tomboy

"This one sure is a fighter, Dad!" yelled sixteen-year-old Amber Kentwood. The small fishing boat rocked back and forth in the water as Amber struggled to reel in the fish. Jim, her dad, had scooted over next to her just in case she needed him. He knew better than to help her if she hadn't asked, though. He was so proud of his little girl. Her long, blond hair was folded up under her baseball cap. She was sweet, pretty, and although delicate looking, she was as tough as nails when she needed to be. She hauled the largemouth bass into the boat with triumph. "Look at it, Dad! It's the biggest one I've ever reeled in by myself!" she exclaimed. "It certainly is a big one!" he said as he hugged his daughter around the shoulders. "That'll feed us all ..." Jim began. They both stopped smiling and were momentarily quiet. "That'll feed both of us." Jim corrected himself. Amber gave her father a hug, and held on to him for a minute. It had been six months since Mrs. Kentwood had died. They both were still having trouble accepting it, as anyone who had been through a similar situation would understand.

Jim started the trolling motor on the boat and headed toward the spot where they had put in. "It sure is quiet on the old Cheyenne River today, don't you think?" he asked Amber. "I hadn't really noticed until you mentioned it," she said. He knew the sounds of the Cheyenne River well. He had been taking the same trip from Faith, South Dakota to this spot for twenty-five years now. He had been going with his father and grandfather for as long as he could remember. His grandfather had died before Amber was born. His father had died four years ago. At least Amber had gotten to go fishing with him for several years. "I guess we'll still be coming out here when you have kids." said Jim, thinking out loud. Amber looked up from the water. She had been staring at the ripples as the boat chugged along. "Huh?" she asked. "I was just thinking about my grandfather and my dad. "What were you thinking about them?" she asked. "Our trips out here. I was just thinking that one of these days, we'll be making this trip with your son or daughter." he said. "I'm never getting married!" Amber exclaimed. "I know, I know ... I wasn't either." he said, laughing.

The boat bumped up against the natural, flattened ramp, which was the bank of the river, and he hopped out. He pulled the boat as far onto the bank as he could so Amber could get out easily. Once she was out, they both pulled the boat further up. Jim unfastened the small motor, and put it, along with the battery, in the back of his old SUV. Amber collected the fishing poles, tackle boxes, and her prize catch. They both pushed the small boat on top of the SUV and strapped it down tight. "Just in time. I think I heard thunder off in the distance." said Amber. Jim listened. "It doesn't sound like thunder to me." he said. The noise got louder. The explosions started. The ground began to shake. The force of the explosions was causing the wind to stir. "Dad, what is it?" yelled Amber over the deafening explosions. Before their very eyes, a section of trees on the bank of the river vanished. There were explosions in the river, causing the water to splash high in the air. Dirt began to rain where explosions strangely erupted from the ground. "I don't know, honey. Let's just get out of here!" Jim exclaimed. As he ran around the SUV, there was an explosion right next to him on the driver's side of the truck. He was thrown several feet away. "Dad!" yelled Amber in fear as she ran to her father. He had blood on his chest. His face was scratched and bruised. "Daddy, are you okay?" she asked frantically. His eyes were not focused, and he didn't move. She started crying and gently shook his shoulder. His eyes came back into focus and he looked at his little girl. He tried to speak, but couldn't. "Come on, Dad, let's get you into the truck." said Amber. It was a struggle, but with Amber's help, he made it into the back of the SUV where he could lie stretched out. He gasped in pain with every sudden move. "I'm going to get you to the hospital, Dad." she said. Before she closed the back of the SUV, Jim managed to speak. "Amber ..." he said in a hoarse, whispery voice. "Amber, come here." She slid over close to him. He motioned for her to come closer so she could hear him better. "Be strong, Amber. I know you can. I love you, honey." he said as his voice faded. "I love you, Daddy." Amber said. Jim Kentwood died. "Daddy? Daddy?" Amber asked softly at first. "Daddy?!" she yelled. She shook his shoulders. "Daddy!" she exclaimed as she began crying. She tried giving him mouth-to-mouth resuscitation, but his lungs would not hold air. She tore his shirt off, revealing a tattered chest. She laid his shirt back over his chest, and hugged him around the neck, and began crying as she held her lifeless father.

5

The Psychopath

"How are you feeling today, Nick?" asked Doctor Wallberg. "Are you being treated properly? Are you getting enough to eat?" Nick Tyler was not looking at Doctor Wallberg. Nick was staring out of the barred window with a dazed look on his face. "Nick?" said Doctor Wallberg. Nick snapped out of his daze and faced the doctor. "Huh? What was that, Doc? I'm sorry." he said, apologetically. She smiled. "I asked you how you were doing and if your accommodations were comfortable." she said. "Oh, yes, I'm fine. Everything's fine ... here at the Phoenix prison." said Nick. Doctor Wallberg frowned. "Nick, you're very lucky you haven't ended up in a real prison instead of this institution. Some people with ... problems ... slip through the system and don't get the proper treatment. They do wrong, and it isn't because they want to do wrong, it's because they didn't know any better. Sometimes, it's a cry for help." the Doctor explained. "Which did I do? Did I not know better, or was I crying for help, Doc?" said Nick. Doctor Wallberg sighed. She couldn't believe this handsome man was in here. He was three years younger than herself.

If he wasn't a patient, on the surface, this man seemed someone that she would date. He was twenty-five, sandy blonde hair, blue eyes, about 5'5", very smart, fairly muscular, with obviously, a good sense of humor. Some of the things they had talked about, that he had done were really quite funny. She, of course, as a professional, had to hold in her laughter. Some of the other things, however, were a little on the dark side and were probably the main reasons he ended up in this institution. "Doc? How're you feeling? Are you being well accommodated?" asked Nick. Doctor Wallberg had been staring down at the floor, thinking. She was embarrassed. She quickly snapped back to attention. "Wanna swap seats, Doc?" he asked. She smiled. "Okay, okay, you made your point. *All* of our minds wander off every now and then." she said. "It just seems to takes yours a little longer to get back." she added. He laughed. That was good. He doesn't think the world revolves around himself. she thought. They both sat quietly for a few moments, then she started back on their daily discussion.

"So, is there anything you would like to talk about today, Nick?" she asked. "Ahh, you mean like the night I went to the grocery store, and was playing bumper cars with the buggy, even though none of the other customers wanted to play, and some of them got very angry?" he asked hurriedly. "We've already talked about that. I want to hear more of your interesting life." she said. She had read the police report of a particularly more violent incident that had happened a few days after the one at the grocery store. She was really looking forward to discussing that one with him, if only she could get him to open up a little more. She needed to get to the bottom of what was causing some of his psychopathic behavior. She was really fond of Nick and really wanted to help him. Some of the things he did, for the most part, were mostly harmless, and sometimes fairly humorous. They could be attributed to someone going a little crazy and blowing off some steam. *Could be.* Some of the other things, however, were extremely dangerous.

Nick was quiet for several moments. "Yeah, I know what you're leading up to, Doc ... the man I put in the hospital." he said. "How do you feel about discussing it?" she asked. Nick looked down at his feet. "Does it matter? If I said that I didn't want to discuss it, could we just forget it?" asked Nick. "Of course, it matters, Nick. I don't want you to talk about anything that makes you feel uncomfortable. We don't have to talk about anything if you don't want to." she said. Nick was, again, quiet for a few moments. "I guess, I feel bad about doing some of the things I did. I guess I'll feel bad talking about them." he said. "Sometimes, talking about something that you did, makes you feel better." she said. "I know! I took Psychology in college! I know I'm a bit bonkers, but I'm not stupid!" exclaimed Nick. Doctor Wallberg sat quietly. "I'm sorry, Doc." said Nick, apologizing for shouting. Nick bowed his head and put it in his hands and began crying, and he wasn't even sure why. Doctor Wallberg pulled her chair next to Nick's and put her arm around his shoulders. "It's okay. It's in the past now. Get it out in the open. Talk to me, Nick. It will make you feel better." she said. "It'll make me feel better, too." she added.

Nick calmed down and regained his composure. He lifted his head up from out of his hands. As he opened his mouth to begin speaking, there was an explosion. The wall behind Doctor Wallberg crumbled, revealing the well-groomed courtyard outside. Dust from the plaster-part of the wall billowed around Nick and Doctor Wallberg. They could hear screams began erupting randomly, throughout the institution. "My God, what was that?" asked Doctor Wallberg. Nick was quickly looking around the room, preparing himself for any action he might have to take. He rubbed his eyes to remove the plaster dust that was clinging to his tears. "The heck if I know," said

Nick. Explosions began roaring all around. Although Nick had some mental issues, he was very intelligent and loved science. He made a quick, mental note that the explosions actually sounded more like *implosions*, which could be creating vacuums as a result of the sudden absence of things. There were some flashes of light in the sky. The winds from the powerful explosion blasts began stirring. "Stay here. I'm going to see if I can find out what's going on." said Doctor Wallberg. Ignoring her order, Nick stood up and headed toward the courtyard, outside, through the gaping hole in the building. "Nick, you're not allowed to leave the institution building unaccompanied." she said, authoritatively. "Like heck I'm not. If you stay inside of this crumbling building, you're crazier than I am! Do you think anybody else in this hospital is, at this very moment, getting permission to RUN FOR THEIR LIVES??!!" exclaimed Nick. Before she could answer, there was another explosion very near. Part of the ceiling came down on top of Dr. Wallberg, scattering more plaster dust. Nick rushed to the pile of debris. "Doc?" asked Nick. Doctor Wallberg weakly opened her eyes. "Guess I should've run with you, while I had the chance, huh?" she said. Nick forced a smile. She didn't sound too good. "I'm going to find help for you. Will you be okay, Doc?" he asked. "I'm okay, Nick." she said. She slowly closed her eyes. "I think you will be too ... in time." she added. It was her last breath. "Doc?" said Nick. He struggled with the beams and debris that were on top of her. They were much too heavy for him. He felt her pulse. There was none. The pile of unmovable rubble prevented any attempt at CPR. He gently brushed the hair away from her forehead and kissed her there, then ran out of the building.

Nick had to maneuver around small fires, that had erupted from the explosions that were still going on all around him. He ran straight toward the entrance that he had first come through when he arrived at the institution. He stopped three times to try and help some people that were lying on the ground. It was already too late for them. As Nick ran by the entrance, he caught a glimpse of the welcome sign he had seen when he was first brought to the hospital and chuckled. It read:

PHOENIX MENTAL INSTITUTION

A Safe Place

Nick ran across the road and cut through a sparse patch of woods, and came out in a residential neighborhood. There were many beautiful homes. One of them was on fire. As he ran up the street, he saw a realty sign in front of the biggest house in sight. It was a brick house. He ran to it and peeked through a window. There was no furniture. The house was vacant. He ran around to the rear of the house. The house was two-story, and he was happy to see that there were glass doors at the back to the basement. He glanced around quickly and spotted a pile of rocks at the edge of the backyard. He ran to them and grabbed a big one from the pile. He ran back to the glass doors and threw it hard against them. They shattered with ease. Nick ducked through the broken glass. He figured he would be safest here in the basement, so he looked around for a comfortable spot. He found a musty, old blanket in what evidently was the wash-room, sat in the corner, and covered himself completely with it. All he could do now was wait.

6

The Actress

The young man was running hard. He darted back and forth in-between people as he ran up the crowded sidewalk. It was very hot in Hollywood, California. Sweat poured from the young man's brow. He was clinching a white, plastic bag in one hand. He turned the corner onto an alleyway and ran up a set of stairs. He ran down a long hallway and stopped at a small booth. The guard inside the booth looked at him with pity and shook his head slowly. "I'm tellin' ya." the young man said to the guard. The guard pressed a button, and the young man pulled the handle of a door with 'Studio 6' labeled on it. It opened sluggishly, and the young man darted in. He walked swiftly past the commotion of people that were talking and shuffling about, carrying different pieces of filming equipment and handling props that were scattered around. He opened another door with the name 'Tracey Blaine' labeled on it. There was an attractive redhead, wearing a long, sleek, dark blue dress, sitting in front of a large, lit, vanity table and mirror. Her low-cut strapless dress didn't leave much to the imagination. Her lips were glistening with the reddest color anyone could have possibly imagined. "Sorry, I'm late. I had to go four blocks to find what you wanted." said the young man. She turned on her swivel chair. "You're fired. Get out." she said, as she turned back to face the mirror. "But, Ms. Blaine! I just said that I had to ..." the young man began. "I asked for my lunch thirty minutes ago! I don't want to have to wait around all day!" she said, interrupting the young man. "It's only been twenty minutes! I had to run four blocks going and back!" he exclaimed. She turned and faced the young man once again. "Are you hard of hearing? Get out or I'll have you thrown out!" she yelled as she snatched the bag from his hands. He opened his mouth to speak, but decided not to. He turned to leave, then stopped at the door, thinking. He turned back around and walked back to where she sat at her vanity. She was already raising a forkful of Greek salad to her mouth. He grabbed her wrist. He forced her to lower the fork back down to the plastic bowl. He shook the forkful of salad back into the bowl. He covered the bowl, and placed it back in the bag. He headed to the door carrying *his* Greek salad. Tracie had been too stunned at his unbelievable actions to try to stop him. "You'll regret that, little man." Tracey said. "Having regrets lets us know that we're human, you witch!" he snapped back. He opened the door and looked back once more. "And by the way, the name's Rick, Rick Conners, *little* woman." he said. He slammed the door as he strolled out of the studio.

Tracey Blaine snatched the phone up from the top of her vanity. "Hello, Dave? My personal assistant has just insulted and threatened me. See to it that he gets a good farewell party. He's wearing a green shirt and blue jeans. He's headed out of the studio now. Thanks a mill." she said to the man on the telephone. She hung up the phone, walked over to her window, and pulled the curtain aside. She had a perfect view of where Rick would be coming out. "You're going to see that being human also means getting beat down when you mess with Tracey Blaine," she said aloud.

Rick descended the stairs, then headed down the alleyway. As he approached the corner of the building, two large men with muscular builds rounded it and entered the alleyway. He knew immediately what was going on. He had heard the stories of what happens when you cross the ill-tempered actress, but he had really needed the job. He ran back to the stairs. As he began his ascent, he felt a sudden pull around his ankle. He grabbed the railing of the stairway and held on. He was pulled all the way back to the bottom. His hands slammed against the pavement as he was pulled from the end of the railing. One of the men picked him up by his shirt, and threw him further toward the building and away from the stairs. He landed hard on his back. The wind was knocked out of him momentarily. As he was lying on his back, looking straight up, toward the building tops, he spotted Tracey looking down at him from her window.

He could hear the two men laughing. He knew they were going to toy with him before they did any real damage. He knew they were going to enjoy it. He also knew there was absolutely nothing he could do to stop it. Rick staggered to his feet. He looked up at Tracey, then got into a defensive stance. The two men began walking toward Rick. The man on the left suddenly flickered and disappeared. The man on the right slumped to the ground with his body cut cleanly in half, bilaterally. A pool of blood formed around what was left of the man. Rick actually heard Tracey scream all the way from her elevated room, just before the explosions started. He glanced up once more and saw that Tracey had left the window. He ran from the building and disappeared down a nearby alleyway.

Tracey ran from her dressing room, screaming hysterically. Everyone in the studio stopped what they were doing and got quiet as their attention turned to the screaming actress. As a few people went to see what was wrong with her, the building shook. Explosions started booming all around. Windows began imploding, spraying glass into the studio. Other people now began screaming and running toward exit doors. No one was concerned with Tracey anymore. They had their own survival in mind. Tracey was knocked down and stepped on in the frenzy. She kept calling out for someone to help her. Four minutes after the explosion had started, Tracey found that she was alone in the studio. She was sobbing with fear and self-pity. Tracey was draped in uncertainty as to what she should do, with no one there to aid her. She went to an interior building wall and leaned her back against it and slid down to a sitting position. She wrapped her arms around her head in a protective gesture and began crying, desperately hoping for the noise and destruction to stop.

7

The Kid

Two young men walked up the sidewalk toward the big double doors, that were the front entrance to Oakwood High School. As Keith Westman reached to open the door, both doors swung open, and two older students pushed through, knocking Keith and his friend, Danny Grant, onto the hard sidewalk. The two older students didn't pay any attention to Keith and Danny, they just kept walking. "You fart-breath creeps!" yelled Danny to the two rude students. The taller of the two students put his hand on the other one's shoulder, so as to stop him. The two twelfth graders turned around. The taller of the two was Reggie Jenkins, the biggest trouble-maker in the whole school. The other twelfth grader was one of his flunkies, Barry Greene. "What did you say, butt-lick?" asked Reggie. Keith and Danny were collecting their books from the sidewalk. As they stood up, Danny said "I said you were fart-breath creeps." Reggie looked from Danny to Keith. "And what about you, nerd-ball?" Reggie said to Keith. Danny looked over at Keith, to find him smiling. "I've got to agree with Danny, Reggie. But there is hope.

Fart-breath is caused by eating farts. Stop eating farts, and you've got it whipped." snapped Keith. Keith could no longer contain his laughter. Danny couldn't either. Both began laughing hard. "You two are the only things that are gonna get whipped!" yelled Reggie as he and Barry began pursuit of the smaller ninth graders. Keith slung one of the double doors open, and Danny followed him through it. Reggie and Barry were only seconds behind them. They had to push their way through the students that were out in the hall, mingling, and preparing for their fourth-period classes. Finally, they reached their homeroom class. They flew through the door, pulling it closed behind them. The teacher was not there yet. No one was there yet. Danny ran for the door. He reached it just as it began opening. Reggie and Barry stepped through, closing it behind them.

"I'll scream." said Danny. "Oh, yes. You are gonna scream, you little turd. Everyone will soon know what a chicken you are." said Reggie. "Listen, Reggie. Be big about this. We didn't hurt you. You already got the better of us when you knocked us down outside." said Keith. "But you insulted me." said Reggie. "Okay, we apologize." said Keith. "Not me!" said Danny. "Too late, anyway, Grant!" said Reggie as he began walking toward Danny. Barry rushed Keith, grabbed him, and held his arms behind his back, so he would not try to interfere. Reggie smashed Danny in the face with his fist, not even using full force. Keith's tough friend swayed but did not fall. "Stop!" yelled Keith as he struggled to break free from Barry. Danny lunged toward Reggie, but the bigger boy's longer reach hit him again before he could approach, this time busting his nose. Keith started yelling for help. Reggie turned toward Barry and said "Keep that little degenerate quiet!" Barry got Keith into a headlock and held his arm against his mouth, so he could not yell. As Reggie turned back toward Danny, he felt a jolt of pain in the groin. Danny had managed to launch his foot between Reggie's legs and kicked him as hard as he could. Reggie was hopping around, holding his crotch and shouting expletives at Danny. Danny headed toward Barry. The door to the classroom opened. Mr. Branton stepped in. "What's going on here?" he demanded. Barry released Keith. Danny and Keith ran toward the door. "Forget him!" yelled Reggie as he let go of his crotch and ran toward Keith and Danny. Mr. Branton stepped between Reggie and his targets. Reggie grabbed the elderly Mr. Branton and slung him against the wall. Mr. Branton fell to the floor, with his head seeping blood. Keith and Danny looked down at Mr. Branton with shock and disbelief at what they had just witnessed. "Come on, Barry!" yelled Reggie. Barry was shocked too, but as always, he did what Reggie told him. Danny snapped out of his state of shock and pulled Keith toward the door. "Keith, run!" he yelled. They ran from the room, with Reggie and Barry pursuing them once again.

Halfway down the hall, Keith stopped abruptly. "What are you doing?" asked Danny. Keith pointed to the Chemistry Lab. Danny nodded and they darted into the Chemistry Lab. There currently weren't any classes, so the lab was empty. Keith turned the thumb-turn to the heavy lock on the door. Reggie and Barry were quickly banging on the door, only a few seconds later. "You little ankle biters!" yelled Reggie. Reggie instructed Barry to stay at the door, as he ran down the hall and headed outside. "Danny, here's what we'll need ..." said Keith as he started spouting off things for Danny to help him find.

Reggie reached the outside of the Chemistry Lab. He quickly scanned the length of the room from the outside and spotted one of the lab's push-out windows barely cracked open. He grinned and headed for it. As he pulled the window open, he jumped backward with a yell. Keith and Danny had wired the window to initiate contact into a nearby power receptacle when pulled on. "You brats!" yelled Reggie with fury as he regained his footing. He picked up a rock and hurled it through another window. He broke all the pieces out, then pulled himself through. He slowly looked around. He saw a storage closet at the back of the room, with the lights turned out. A cursory glance led him to believe that could be the only place they could be hiding. He went to the door and let Barry in, closing and locking the door behind him. "This time, Barry, I want them *dead.*" said Reggie. "Man, I don't think ..." started Barry. Reggie grabbed Barry by the collar and slung him up against the wall. "Are you with me, or against me, Barry?" Reggie said in a whisper. Barry managed to stutter out that he was definitely *with* Reggie. "Go flush them out." said Reggie as he pointed to the dark storage closet. Barry walked slowly to the back of the room at the storage closet entrance and then stopped. He looked back at Reggie. "Go!" commanded Reggie. Barry stepped inside the closet. There was enough light filtering in for him to see the closet's light switch. He flipped it. There was a blinding flash and a large puff of smoke. Barry stumbled back holding his eyes, nose, and mouth. He crashed down onto a chair. Suddenly, there was a savage cry behind Reggie and he whirled around in time to see two cabinet doors swing open with Keith and Danny running out of them screaming. They held beakers in their hands. They sloshed the contents of the beakers into Reggie's face. He screamed as the acid began to burn. He couldn't see, so he began blindly swinging his fists. Danny and Keith headed for the door. Barry stepped in front of them. His face was red and burned, with smoke coming from his hair. They turned back around and ran back into the room. Reggie was heading right toward them swinging a long, glass tube. As the tube began its descent upon Keith and Danny, it disappeared, along with Reggie. So did many of the desks and chairs. An entire wall disappeared. They turned toward Barry. The only thing left of him was the stubs of his feet. They looked at each other and then ran frantically through the opening leading to the hallway, where the wall section had just occupied moments before. They could hear the screams and cries of other school kids and faculty begin mounting. "What's going on?" yelled Danny as they ran down the hallway toward one set of many exit doors.

They were outside, running at top speed. Cars, people, trees, and structures were disappearing all around them. Some of the vanishings were partial, and some encompassed the entire subject. Explosions started rippling all around. It seemed as though nothing was immune to whatever was happening. They headed toward the thick, unkept patch of woods behind the school. They ran deep into the woods. In their minds, they thought that this might be an escape from whatever was happening, and maybe they would not have to witness any more of the destruction. Deep down, both boys figured that they probably weren't any safer, but it just *felt* safer. They sat beside each other up against a large Oak tree. They pulled their limbs up as close to their bodies as they could. "I'm scared." said Keith. "Me too," said Danny. They scooted closer together, closed their eyes, and waited as much of their town and the inhabitants of Colfax, Washington began disappearing all around them.

8

The Settling

Marty slowly lifted his head and listened. Nothing. The explosions had subsided. He waited for the noises of people crying and panicking. Nothing. *I'm in a closet, in a café. I can't hear anything in here. Everyone's outside.* Marty thought. He stood up slowly, opened the door, and stepped out of the closet. The closet was all that was left of the building he was in. What was left of New York was in ruins. Marty wasn't much in the kindness department, but he was a good-looking man. He was thirty-four years old. He had brown hair that he kept perfectly styled. He was 5' 9" and very solid looking. The look of a high-tech salesman depicted him to a tee. He looked strange, standing amidst the devastation. There were small, scattered fires burning off in the distance. There were a few scattered bodies. None were alive. "Hello!" yelled Marty. His voice mysteriously boomed out and echoed through the ruins of what was left of The Big Apple.

* * * * *

Dust lightly floated down the old stairway of the courthouse.

Mandy couldn't see the dust, but she could feel it as she breathed. "Maybe it's over." she said. She gently squeezed the old man's hand. She received no indication of his condition back from him. She gently shook the old man on the shoulder. He fell over in a slump. "No." she said with a quivering voice. She knelt down and felt his pulse. There was none. She began to softly cry. She was still sniffling when she collected what was left of her robe and put it in her purse. She slowly began climbing the stairs. She emerged from the courthouse to find vast destruction and occasional lifeless bodies littering the streets. Most of the buildings were in ruins. A few of them were on fire. All she heard was the slight rustling of the wind, and some crackling from the fires. There were no signs of any life, except for her own. Mandy began scouting out what was left of the town.

* * * * *

The old pickup truck's frame protested with loud squeaks and pings as Briggs went through a ditch on the side of the long road to go around one of many clusters of cars that were dotted along the highway. Almost all of the cars had no drivers. Some were burning. Some were cut in half. The preacher would actually laugh whenever he saw a particularly interesting mangled, dead body. There was death and destruction for as far as he could see. He was grinning from ear to ear. Until he topped the next hill. He almost drove off of the road he got such a surprise. There was a white vehicle, kind of like a van, only much longer, heading toward him. All of the windows of the vehicle were tinted black. It had what appeared to be a small satellite dish on top of it, with other antennas mounted on top. It came to a stop, and three figures dressed in white radiation-type suits and protective helmets, with tinted face shields, got out. They were each carrying and operating hand-held devices. Their attention was intently focused on Briggs and his truck as he slowed to a stop.

* * * * *

The sounds of destruction finally subsided. It had felt like an eternity to Amber. It didn't matter anyway. Her father was dead. He was all that mattered in her world. She thought she had finished crying until she had climbed into the driver's seat of the old SUV. There was a picture of her and Jim that had been on the keychain for the past three years. They were holding a nice-sized Bass. Now, she kept visualizing her father's lifeless body in the back of the truck. She began to cry again. *Be strong, Amber. I know you can. I love you, honey.* Her father's last words echoed in her mind. She forced herself to stop crying. She started the SUV and headed in the direction they had come. She had only had her license for a few months, and she wasn't sure if she would be able to get back home without some help. As she emerged from the wooded area, she turned left on the paved road. She turned on the radio to see if she could find out what had happened. There was static on all of the stations. As Amber began to see the chaos and destruction, she quickly realized that she may not be getting the help she was hoping for.

* * * * *

Nick jumped. He felt suffocated. He began thrashing his limbs frantically. He finally got the blanket pulled off of his head. He had fallen asleep in the cool, musty basement after he had covered himself with the blanket. He stood up and walked outside, through the busted glass doors. He was surprised to find large holes in the rear of the house. "Boy, I can sleep through anything." he said aloud. He walked around to the front. He saw that the house that had been burning was now in ashes. There were only two houses in the neighborhood that were standing and the one he had chosen was one of them.

Not really knowing what to do, Nick headed back toward the hospital. The woods he had gone through looked as if a tornado or hurricane had hit them. As he approached the hospital, his spirits rose. It looked as if there was already some type of emergency vehicle there. A large white vehicle with a small satellite dish and several antennas was parked in front of the hospital amidst the wreckage. He hurried to see if he could help. As he came around the vehicle, he was shocked at what he saw.

* * * * *

The building stopped shaking and Tracey gradually began to gain control of herself. She sat up and looked around the abandoned studio. There was broken equipment, broken panels that had fallen from the ceiling, and shattered glass everywhere. The wind blowing through the broken windows blew loose papers around the room. One of these papers brushed by Tracey and she let out a shrill scream. She was a bundle of nerves. She crawled over to one of the windows and looked out. The city was on fire. Many buildings had toppled and fallen. She could see that smoke was coming out of the bottom of the building that she was in. She shakily gained her feet. Her body ached from the scratches and bruises caused by people stepping on her. She walked as quickly as she could to the door and walked through to the hallway. There was blood streaking down the entire length of the floor to the stairway. She walked the hallway, deliberately looking away from the blood. There was smoke coming from under the door at the top of the stairway. She touched the doorknob and found it to be very hot. "Ohhhhh." she whimpered in a panic. "Somebody, help me!" she yelled. She ran back down the hall into the studio. She looked down from one of the windows. It was impossible to climb and too far to jump. She began yelling out of the window. She yelled until her throat was sore and hoarse. Tracey slumped down to the floor and began sobbing.

Tracey had only been sobbing for a few minutes when she thought she heard something and looked up. She saw two figures dressed in white radiation-type suits and protective helmets in the studio walking toward her. She jumped up with joy and ran to them. "Oh, thank God! I thought I was going to die in this place!" she exclaimed. The figures did not respond but motioned her toward the door. She happily took the lead.

Outside, Tracey found herself standing beside a white vehicle. She saw a third figure examining the body of one of the men Dave had sent after Rick Conners. He discontinued his examination and joined Tracey and the two others. "Were we nuked from a war?" Tracey asked hesitantly. There was no reply. A large side door on the vehicle opened up from bottom to top. Tracey looked at her three rescuers and confirmed that they wanted her to get in the vehicle. She did so. The three figures followed.

* * * * *

"I think it's over." said Keith looking in the direction of the schoolyard. Keith was fifteen years old and had an average build for a young man of his age. He was very clean but didn't give his straight, black hair any special grooming considerations. "Danny?" said Keith. He looked back and was staring blankly at where Danny had been only a short time earlier. Now, there was no trace of him. "Danny!" Keith yelled. "This ain't funny!" he yelled. Keith stood up and jogged through the woods toward the school. He stopped dead in his tracks. There was no longer a school. Just a big, dirt crater where it had once been. Keith began running as fast as he could. His house was only a few miles away. As he ran down the sidewalk, dodging the piles of debris and wreckage, Keith noticed that there was no one in sight. He was the only thing moving except for various smoke plumes off in the distance, and the rustle of wind-blown leaves through nearby trees.

9

Collection Agency

Tracey sat down on a cushioned bench inside of the pristine white vehicle. Two of the figures sat down on a bench on the opposite side of Tracey. The third went through a door to the front of the vehicle. The vehicle began moving. Some of the scientific equipment mounted inside rattled around as it turned a corner. The ride smoothed out as they straightened up. The two figures opposite Tracey removed their helmets. One was a man, the other a woman. "Can you tell me what's happened?" Tracey asked. The woman turned away from Tracey, without as much as an acknowledgment. "Ma'am, we aren't allowed to discuss anything. Please just sit back and refrain from touching anything." said the man. Tracey looked back at the woman. The woman turned away again, avoiding eye contact with her. "What's wrong?" Tracey asked. Neither of them replied.

* * * * *

Two of the figures approached Preacher Briggs, who had stayed in his vehicle. "I do believe the Lord has come!" exclaimed Briggs as the figures stopped next to his truck. The third figure disappeared into the white vehicle. "Sir, please get out of the vehicle." said the suited figure that was closest to John's door. Briggs remained quiet. "Sir, get out of the vehicle." repeated the same figure, a little more sternly. "Can't do that, son." said Preacher Briggs. The figure reached in through John's open window to attempt to switch off the truck. The Preacher stomped down on the accelerator. The old pickup lurched forward. The figure had initially grabbed onto John's arm but then found that it had got entangled and he was dragged along with the truck. The truck slammed into the side of the white vehicle. The figure that was dragged along with John was thrown to the side. The other figure ran to the truck and opened John's door, and began attempting to pull the preacher from the truck. The figure that had been thrown to the ground stood up, shook off his trauma, and began helping the other figure pull on John. The two of them finally managed to get him out of his truck. They soon learned that was their mistake. John slung one of the figures off of him. He hurled the remaining one up against the side of his truck. The other one jumped on John's back from behind. John turned around. With his back to the white vehicle, he heaved his body backward and slammed the figure into it. It had knocked the figure's helmet off. Briggs could now see a man with a busted nose. He headed back toward his truck. The third figure that had been inside of the white vehicle now came out. The figure was carrying a device in his gloved, left hand. With his right hand, he grabbed the back of John's shirt and pulled him backward down to the ground. The preacher was really surprised at the strength of this other figure. The figure jumped on top of him. He seemed to be trying to stick the device into John's ear. John was struggling to hold his arm away. He could see the strained look of himself in the reflection of the black plastic face shield on the white helmet. Soon, John's arms began to fatigue.

His strength seemed to be no match for the strength of the figure
who was now trying to stick what looked like a large syringe into
his ear. As the device got closer, Briggs began to hear a buzz coming
from it. Just as his strength was giving out, the figure was knocked
off of him. There was a shot. John looked to his side to see that
his assailant was motionless. The man with the broken nose was
standing over the dead figure, holding the revolver that John had
kept in his dash. "No more." said the man, as if exhausted. Preacher
Briggs slowly gained his feet. "Are you okay?" asked the man as
he offered his hand to John. The preacher grabbed his revolver as
the man helped him up. He stared at the smoking revolver in his
hands. He pointed it at the man with the broken nose and shot him
twice in the chest. He turned to see the other figure scrambling to
his feet. John emptied the remaining three rounds into the figure.
"I am now." he said, breathing deeply. Briggs began laughing in his
deep voice. He got back into his truck and drove around the white
vehicle. He continued down the road.

　　＊ ＊ ＊ ＊ ＊

The tires squalled from the sudden stop of the SUV. Amber's
heart was racing. She barely got stopped before she plummeted into
the crater below. The crater was several hundred feet in diameter. It
was about a hundred feet deep. She looked down into the crater and
could see mankind's underground infrastructure of various utilities.
Pipes, conduits, and cables of different sizes, colors, and materials
that conveyed the various items that were typical of modern society.
Strangely, the cut of the crater and the cuts of the utilities seemed
to perfect, as if done with a laser. She slowly lowered her head onto
the steering wheel and sighed with despair. She sat quietly for a few
minutes, then backed up and turned the SUV around. She headed
in the opposite direction.

As she looked at the homes and buildings destroyed, she began to
fully realize the extent of devastation that had occurred. She saw no

living creature along the road. She had traveled this direction before with her father and remembered the scenery. Most of the stores that had dotted the roadside were gone. Some were still burning.

She drove on into the night, stopping only to rest. After many hours of driving, she came to her state's capital, Pierre, South Dakota. Pierre looked as if it was hit by an earthquake. Amber sleepily drove around looking for a place to spend the night. She was forced to turn around on many of the streets that she entered due to wreckage blocking the way. She finally found a hotel that looked like it was in fairly good shape. She pulled the SUV right up onto the sidewalk at the front entrance. She slowly and tiredly walked to the glass doors and then turned back and faced the SUV. "Goodnight Daddy." she said. She went into the hotel.

Although old, the hotel was very nice. It had a large, open lobby with luxurious furnishings. She found the front desk and went behind it. She got the first key she could find to a room on the bottom floor. She was grateful that it still used standard keys, otherwise, she may have found herself sleeping in the lobby. She had the key for room number three. Before she went to the room, she carefully used the stairs and climbed them up to the fifth floor. She walked to one of the large windows at the end of the fifth-floor hallway. She looked out over the city. The moon and stars were pretty and bright, but the city looked weird in almost total darkness. She counted eleven places that she could see that still had lighting. As she was about to turn away, her heart caught in her throat. She quickly looked back out the window. It was very faint and very far off, but it was there. There was a light moving off in the distance. Her first reaction was to go jump into the SUV and head in that direction. However, her common sense caught her. It would take her many, many hours to get to where the moving light was, even if it was heading in her direction. That is if her wonderful sense of direction could even find it. Not to mention, the new dangers along the roadways with all the destruction. Besides, she was dead tired. Amber found it hard to believe that she would be the only survivor of some kind of war or catastrophe anyway. She took one more look at the light, then headed back down the stairs.

Her room was very comfortable, but it could've been cooler. The windows didn't open and although she was certain she was alone, she was too scared to leave her door open. She made sure the door was locked. She pulled the drapes open just enough to let in a little moonlight and starlight. She made her way to the bathroom, realizing she would have to use it in the dark. She was so sleepy, that she almost fell asleep on the toilet.

As she curled up in the middle of the bed, her mind started drifting as she began to lose consciousness. She was hot, and she was again thinking about why she had shut and locked the door. She had been scared because of all the people that must have died. She also remembered a wise saying that her father had once said to her. *Amber, it's not the dead people you have to worry about ... it's the live ones.* It was all very sarcastic. She realized that her father was the only dead body she'd seen up close since everything that had happened. She finally slept.

* * * * *

Marty Maxx had been wandering the deserted streets of New York City for hours. He was hot and sweaty from his time of walking. It was impossible to navigate a vehicle through the areas he had visited due to the cluttered streets of destruction. He was tired. It was getting dark and he was only now thinking of where he was going to stay for the night. He also realized that he was very hungry and hadn't eaten in a long while.

Pierre D'avandos was a fine restaurant for the upper class. Most of New York had lost electricity. Pierre D'avandos was one of the eating establishments that had a backup generator. He went to the back of the restaurant toward the kitchen. His stomach turned as he entered a hallway. There were two severed legs in the middle of the hallway. He looked away as he walked around the limbs and kept his distance. Marty found the freezers in the back, next to the kitchen. He carefully used a pan from the kitchen as a chock for the door. He went inside and looked around. He found boxes of "We use fresh - never frozen" steaks, vegetables, and pastries. He collected what he thought he would eat, and went to the kitchen. He started the oven and placed his steak in the microwave to begin to thaw. He was in the kitchen for almost an hour preparing his supper. He finally finished, got some colas from the refrigerator, and eagerly headed to the dining area, to stretch out, rest, and enjoy his meal.

As Marty entered the dining room, he almost dropped his dinner and drinks. There were two suited figures standing just inside the entrance to the restaurant as if they were waiting for him. Marty slowly and cautiously walked behind a table. "You guys are military, right?" he asked hesitantly. "Sir, please come with us." the figure on the left said. "Now, wait. I've been through the wringer today! I'm tired and hungry. Can't I eat first?" asked Marty pleadingly. The two figures approached Marty. The one in front locked his hand onto Marty's arm. "Come this way, please." said the figure as he began leading Marty toward the door. Marty carefully held onto his plate of food and cola.

Outside, Marty was led to a large, white vehicle with half-tracks. It had a blade on the front that looked similar to that of a snow-plow. "I've never seen one of these before." said Marty. One of the figures climbed the small ladder that led into the back of the vehicle and then motioned for the things Marty was carrying. Reluctantly, Marty reached up and handed the plate and cola to the figure. He then climbed up himself. The figure with Marty pressed a button, and the hatch they had entered closed. The other figure climbed another ladder that led into the cab of the vehicle. Marty was seated on a comfortable, white bench. The figure sat on a similar bench opposite Marty. He removed his helmet. As the vehicle began moving, Marty started eating his food. "What's happened out there?" Marty asked through a mouthful of food. "I don't know." responded the man blankly. "Are you with the military?" Marty asked. "No." said the man, flatly. "Who are you with?" asked Marty. "All of your questions will be answered later. Now please remain quiet, and finish your meal. We have a long ride." snapped the man. "Sorry." Marty said. The vehicle moved on into the night. Marty gulped his food down, then stretched out on the bench and slept. He was awakened a few times from the clash of metal on metal as the vehicle cleared its way through heavy debris.

※ ※ ※ ※ ※

Keith's house was one of the few that were left standing in his neighborhood. He slowly climbed the front porch steps, and then sat down at the top of them. He rested and let his heart rate slow down from the long run home. He was much calmer now. His Mom hadn't planned to go anywhere today, so Keith figured that there was a good chance that she was safely inside the house. After he was breathing regularly once again, he unlocked the front door and went in.

"Mom?" Keith said as he walked toward the kitchen. She was not in the kitchen. "Mom?" Keith said louder as he headed for the living room. She was not there either. "Mom!" Keith shouted as he ran upstairs to his parents' bedroom. She was not in the bedroom. Keith searched every room in the house. His mother was nowhere to be found. He picked up the phone to try calling his father's office. The line was dead. Keith sat down at the kitchen table and put his head in his arms and started to cry. He knew deep down that the chances of either parent being alive were next to none. He forced himself to accept the fact that he had not seen another living creature since he came out of the woods at school. He went through several fits of crying before he had no tears left. He had not given up, but he had come to grips with the facts that surrounded him. One thing he knew for sure was that for the time being, he was on his own.

Keith went to his own bedroom. He got his backpack out of his closet. Keith collected various items from around his room to put in it. He packed away a small blanket, a knife, some extra clothes, a picture of his parents, a portable radio, a flashlight, and some BBs for his BB gun. He carried the backpack and his BB gun to the kitchen and began making some sandwiches. He took some sandwiches, a box of cereal, a box of crackers, the remainder of a loaf of bread, a jar of peanut butter, and a box of snack cakes. He stuffed all of the food, some silverware, and a milk jug that he had rinsed out and filled with ice and water down into his backpack. He left a note on the kitchen table, just in case. He then went outside.

Keith had never been one to sit and wait. All he could think to do now was head to his father's office. It was almost an hour's drive, so there was no telling how long it was going to take him to ride on his bicycle. He secured the straps of the backpack to the front handlebars of his bicycle. He slid his BB gun snugly under the straps, between the backpack and the handlebars. He got on his bike and headed down the street.

* * * * *

As Preacher Briggs drove away, the figure that had been trying to stick a device into his ear began crawling toward the wrecked vehicle. The figure moaned and groaned from the bullet wound as he pulled himself up the ladder into the cab of the vehicle. The small satellite dish on top of the vehicle began turning in circles. A large antenna raised a few feet in the air.

* * * * *

When Amber awakened in the morning, all of the events of the previous day came rushing back into her thoughts. The destruction, the loneliness, and her dad. Mostly thoughts of her dad flooded her mind. She was very surprised that she did not begin crying. There was a pain in her stomach. She was very hungry, but the pain was mostly from the emptiness she now had from losing her father. She stopped staring at the ceiling and got up from bed. She unlocked the door and went out.

Amber wandered around the hallways until she found the snack machines. She went outside and got the tire tool from the SUV. When she came back, she repeatedly beat the snack machine with the tire tool and soon found that she was not going to be breaking into it. She disappointedly went back outside and got into the SUV. She started it up and left the hotel.

She remembered the lights she saw before she went to sleep, but the first thing on her mind was getting something to eat. As she headed across the city, in the direction she had seen the lights, she spotted the logo of a fast-food restaurant. She wanted to speed but knew it would be dangerous with the conditions as they were.

As was the hotel, the restaurant was deserted as well. Amber walked behind the counter and collected a few bags full of hamburgers and cheeseburgers to take with her. As she walked back out of the restaurant, she thought with the heat as it is, stuff is going to really start spoiling soon. Her stomach lurched as she suddenly thought of her father. She really needed to bury him. After she ate, she drove around looking for some sort of hardware store. She found a popular big box hardware store. Well, it was half of one. She hoped the remaining half had what she needed. She went inside and came back out a few minutes later carrying a shovel. She put it in the back of the SUV beside her Father. She drove around looking for a cemetery. After a little while, she finally gave up. She began heading back in the direction of where she had seen the lights.

She had driven for an hour when the city limits sign came into view. She wondered if she was on the same road that whoever was out last night had been on. It was getting much hotter. Amber pulled off to the side of the road. She put her head against the steering wheel and sighed. She got out of the SUV and got the shovel out of the back. She walked twenty feet from the edge of the road to where it seemed the dirt was the softest. She made a mental note to write down where she was so she could always visit her father if that was in her future. She began digging Jim Kentwood a grave.

* * * * *

Marty had been traveling for two days in the white vehicle. The only times that they had stopped was to use the bathroom. He, along with the suited man that rode with him, had been eating food-paste as Marty imagined the first astronauts ate. Marty noticed that they had been traveling in a southerly direction. As the vehicle came to a stop, Marty stood up. A green light in the ceiling of the vehicle came on. "Sir, please sit down." said the suited man. "I thought we were going to the bathroom." said Marty as he sat back down. "Not this time." responded the suited man. He walked over to Marty and fastened his wrist to the railing of the cushioned bench with restraints that were very similar to handcuffs. "What's this all about?" Marty asked hysterically. "Sir, don't be alarmed. We have another passenger to pick up. This is just procedure." said the suited man as he put his helmet on. He walked to the back of the vehicle and picked up a small device that had a strong resemblance to a gun. He pressed the button for the door and it hissed as it opened. Before it closed, Marty got a glimpse of the outside area. There were many bodies lining the streets. Much more than in New York. He wondered why.

* * * * *

"Hello? Is there anyone out there? Please respond." Mandy Richards said into the microphone. She had taken a gas-powered generator from what was left of the local hardware store and was powering a small ham radio setup she found at the police station. She remembered this from the last time she was at the police station. As much as she didn't like the memory, she knew this would be the best place to be in an emergency situation. It would have made her feel better if someone was alive to keep her company, though. "Am I the only survivor of some kind of this?" Mandy said into the microphone. "Ma'am, please come with me." said a voice from the hallway, just outside of the office she was in. She was very startled and jumped at the sudden outburst. From the pleasant, but firm voice, she guessed that the figure in the white suit was probably from the military and she relaxed. "Guess not." she said in response to her last question. She got up from the desk and switched off the generator. "What's happened?" she asked the figure in the white suit as she walked into the hallway. "Come this way, please." the figure responded. *Definitely military.* Mandy thought. She picked up her pocketbook and followed the figure in the white suit out to the street where a white vehicle waited. "Where are we going?" Mandy asked. The figure pressed a button on the vehicle and the door swung open with a hiss. The figure helped Mandy up the ladder, and into the vehicle. Marty's eyes widened as she entered the vehicle. The figure in the white suit climbed up after her. He pushed the button and the door closed. He walked to the back of the vehicle and placed the device he had taken with him into a compartment. He walked back to the front and removed his helmet. "Please sit down over there, Ma'am." he said, pointing to the bench that Marty was sitting on. Mandy sat down. "Hi. My name's Marty. Marty Maxx." he said as he extended his free, right hand. "Mandy Richards." she said as she shook his hand. "So, are you going to take these handcuffs off now?" Marty asked the man in the white suit. "I'm not allowed." he said. "He's not very talkative, is he?" asked Mandy. "No, he's not." said Marty. The vehicle began moving again.

* * * * *

It was dark, and Keith's bicycle didn't have a headlight on it. Keith could see lights far off in the distance, but there were none near enough so that he could travel without having an accident.

Keith coasted into a familiar convenience store. He rolled his bike into the store with him. He got his flashlight out of his backpack and began to look around. "And I was worried about food." Keith said aloud. He went around the store collecting armfuls of his favorite snacks and beverages. He also got extra batteries for his flashlight and some other supplies he thought may be useful. After he stuffed his backpack to its maximum capacity, he went around the store again, trying to decide what he wanted to eat now. As his flashlight panned across the front counter, something intriguing caught his eye. A nudie magazine. Keith jumped up onto the counter and stretched out his arm toward the magazine rack. He dropped his flashlight. "Crap." he said. He jumped down onto the other side of the counter. He landed on something mushy. He got his flashlight and pointed it down where he was standing. Keith screamed and scrambled back over the counter and ran out the door and leaned back against the wall of the store, panting, no longer imagining what the female anatomy might look like. He had been standing on the clerk. The clerk was covered in blood, and his body had been cleanly cut, bilaterally, with only the right side remaining. Keith calmed down, and then went in quickly and pushed his bike back out. He was going to spend the night somewhere else. Keith began pushing his bike down the dark sidewalk.

* * * * *

Amber had dug almost two feet deep when the white vehicle pulled up beside her SUV. She was too hot and exhausted to be scared. As soon as the two suited figures approached, she raised the shovel defensively. "Who are you?" she asked. "Ma'am, we need for you to come with us." one of the suited figures said through his helmet. "Why?" Amber asked. "This area is not safe." answered a suited figure. "I've got to bury my father first." she said, as she lowered her shovel and continued digging. The suited figures remained motionless for a few moments, and then one of them walked to the front of the vehicle and climbed the ladder that led to the cab. The door opened, and the figure went inside. Less than a minute later, a door on the back of the vehicle opened, and the suited figure came back out carrying two digging tools. He handed one to the other suited figure. They began to help Amber dig her father's grave. An hour later, they were finished. One of the two suited figures helped Amber get her father from the back of the SUV. They carefully placed him in the hole they had dug. Amber removed his wallet, his wedding ring, and his watch. The other suited figure watched them closely. Tears began to form in Amber's eyes as she and the suited figure that had helped her retrieve her father began to fill the hole with dirt. The suited figure that was watching quickly turned away and climbed the ladder up to the cab of the white vehicle. The door opened and the figure went in. When they had finished filling the hole with dirt, Amber bowed her head and closed her eyes. "God, I hope you can hear me. Please take care of my dad and make sure he knows that I love him. Amen." she said. "Amen." said the suited figure. Amber got her keys from the SUV. The keychain and the pictures in her father's wallet might be the only pictures of her and her family that she would ever have. "I'm ready now. Thank you for your help." she said to the suited figure. The suited figure collected the digging tools and then led her into the back of the vehicle. The door hissed as it closed behind them. The suited figure replaced the tools in their proper compartments, and then led Amber to the seating area in the vehicle. She sat on a white, cushioned bench opposite the suited figure. He removed his helmet, and the vehicle began moving. "Where are we going?" Amber asked. "I don't know." said the man as he sighed.

* * * * *

After a few blocks of walking, Keith found another convenience store. He checked it out thoroughly before he settled down to sleep. He didn't want to share his space with any dead bodies. He curled up in a corner as far from the entrance as he could get. He had no way to lock the door. As tired and sleepy as Keith was, it was still several hours before his wandering thoughts would let him rest.

As the first sunlight of morning began filtering through the glass windows and doors, he was awakened by the sound of an engine running. He groggily ran to the door and looked out. There was a large, white vehicle outside with two suited figures climbing down the ladder on the side of it. He grabbed his bike and pushed his way through the door. The suited figures began to approach Keith. "Who are you?" asked Keith. "Sir, we need you to come with us." said one of the figures. "Who are you?" Keith repeated. "That's not important. We need you to come with us." said the other figure as Keith got a running start with his bicycle. The two figures began to run after him. "Wait!" both suited figures yelled at the same time. They barely missed grabbing Keith's shirt by a few inches when he accelerated on his bicycle. The two figures stopped running. They knew they couldn't catch the kid on the speeding bike. "Dang it!" one of the figures yelled. They both hurried back to the white vehicle.

Keith was peddling hard down the next hill on the street when he heard the vehicle approaching from behind. As the vehicle neared, Keith quickly turned onto the next street. The vehicle's tires squalled and the tracks scraped as they took the curve. Keith looked back to see that they were still close and catching him fast. His feet never missed a beat as he peddled the bike. The vehicle was almost at his back tire when he swung the bike off of the street and down an alley. The vehicle locked up its brakes. He looked back to see smoke coming from the front tires of the large vehicle. The vehicle's rear tracks dug ruts into the pavement. He was already a block away before they figured out that they could not fit the vehicle down the narrow alley. "Ha!" Keith laughed as he turned down another alley.

Inside the cab of the vehicle, a screen lit up with a street map of Colfax. There was a stationary green dot representing the white vehicle. There was a flashing red dot two blocks away from the green dot, that represented Keith. There was an information box that kept an updated fix of each dot. It showed latitude, longitude, altitude, speed, and distance. A blue line came out of the green dot and traversed the street map to an intercept course with the flashing red dot. The intercept course was considering the speed and distance of both dots at all times. The vehicle began moving again. After traveling for three blocks around the area, it stopped, and two suited figures got out and began walking up an alley. The vehicle continued on.

Keith turned down another alley. As he got halfway down it, the two suited figures stepped out at the end of it. He pulled his peddles back and skidded sideways, to a stop. The suited figures began jogging toward him. He turned his bike around. As he headed back out of the alley, the white vehicle pulled in front of him at the other end, blocking his exit. "Oh, man!" said Keith. A third suited figure climbed down a ladder from the cab of the vehicle. He turned his bike around and began riding as hard as he could toward the two figures at the other end of the alley. The suited figure at the vehicle pointed something at Keith. A yellow light came from it. Everything turned black, and Keith lost consciousness.

10

Shock

Nick stopped dead in his tracks. Stooped down next to the body of Doctor Wallberg were two suited figures. Their suits were solid white and resembled the radiation suits he had seen in real news stories and science fiction shows. Their helmets were on the ground, beside them. The helmets were made out of the same flexible material as the suits, except for the tinted, black, plastic-looking face shield. The man on the right was short and stocky. He was a white man with red hair and a red beard. The figure on the left was not human. It looked like a monster. Nick was pretty sure he was looking at an Alien. The two figures had been sifting through the debris next to Doctor Wallberg's body. The alien was holding a watch. Nick glanced down at his left wrist to confirm that his watch was missing. It was. It must have slipped off or broken when he was trying to help Doctor Wallberg. The two figures quickly stood up. In a deep, rough, guttural voice, the alien yelled "Get him!"

The man hit Nick like a locomotive. He got the breath knocked out of him when he crashed down onto broken bricks, wood fragments, and other debris. He held on securely to Nick's arms. Nick struggled, but could not break free from the stronger man. The alien approached with a strange-looking device that had a small cone-like extension at the end. He stuck it to Nick's ear. The device emitted a high pitch, and Nick passed out.

The two figures carried Nick up the ladder, and laid him down on the cushioned bench, opposite another cushioned bench. They handcuffed his wrists to the railing of the bench. The alien went through the door that led to the cab of the vehicle. The man removed his helmet and sat down beside a tall, skinny, clean-cut black man who was also wearing a white suit. The doors shut and the vehicle began moving.

11

Transmission Received

The vehicle that Tracey Blaine was in came to a sudden stop. The door separating the cab from the rear of the vehicle opened, and a suited figure, complete with helmet, motioned for the suited man to come forward into the cab. The door shut behind him. "What's wrong?" Tracey asked the suited woman. "I don't know." she replied. After a few moments, the door opened, and the suited man came back into the rear of the vehicle. He handcuffed Tracey to the cushioned bench. "Why did you do that?" Tracey asked him. "Sorry, those were my instructions." When the man sat down, the vehicle began moving again. It was moving much faster than before. Tracey was surprised that such a large vehicle could go as fast as they were now going. "Whose instructions?" Tracey asked. "I can't answer any more of your questions." said the man. "You must not know who you're dealing with here. You two are going to be up to your snot-holes in trouble." Tracey snapped arrogantly. The suited woman jumped up from the bench and grabbed Tracey's shoulders. "You don't know what trouble is yet ... but you're gonna find out!"

she said as she shook Tracey once and then released her. "Now shut your trap before I shut it for you!" she added as she sat back down. Tracey's eyes began to tear up, but she held onto her composure. The suited man looked away as if nothing had happened.

* * * * *

"So, let me guess, you thought you were the last person alive too?" Marty asked Mandy. "I was beginning to think so." said Mandy. "I'm from New York City, New York. Where are you from?" Marty asked. "The big town of Zebulon, Georgia." said Mandy. Marty nodded. "Looking out, I briefly saw what looked like many bodies back there." he said. "I guess in New York, everyone was alive and well? They just came and picked you up for your sparkling conversation?" Mandy snapped. "No, no. That's not what I meant. Most everyone I saw actually *vanished*. I did see some dead bodies, but most of the people around me just vanished into thin air!" exclaimed Marty. Mandy put her hand on her chin and closed her eyes for a few seconds. "Come to think of it, I think I saw some people disappear too. I just figured my eyes were playing tricks on me for being in such a panic. Sorry for snapping." she said. The door separating the cab from the rear of the vehicle opened. "That's enough, you two. No more talking." said the suited man. "Who are these people?" Mandy whispered. "I don't know, but they've got one expensive setup here." responded Marty in a whisper. The door closed, and then the suited man came back to where Mandy and Marty were sitting. He handcuffed Mandy to the other side of the bench. "What in the heck are you doing?" she asked angrily, pulling against the handcuffs. The suited man sat down without responding. "You creep." she said. "Welcome to the club." said Marty, holding his own cuffed arm up for her to see. Their bodies tilted slightly as the vehicle began accelerating.

* * * * *

The vehicle locked up its brakes and skidded for several hundred feet. Wakened by the disturbance, Nick slowly opened his eyes. He felt the vehicle began accelerating backward. It stopped suddenly, then skidded again, and then turned off onto another road, heading in another direction in a big hurry.

He looked around and found that he was inside of some sort of science vehicle. He saw two men sitting across from him. His memories of what had happened flooded in and he tried to sit up. He couldn't move. Both of his hands had been cuffed beside him onto a cushioned bench. "Where am I?" Nick asked the two suited men. "What was that thing?" he asked. The two men remained silent and appeared to be ignoring him. "Oh, I get it. You two are scared of it, whatever *it* is." Nick said as he laughed and tried to provoke a response from either of the two men. "Maybe I am crazy." he said in a low voice. Nick heard a door open from somewhere inside the vehicle. A helmeted, suited figure walked up beside Nick's bench and began looking down at him. Nick hesitated and then said, "You're that thing I was looking at." The suited figure removed his helmet. In the same deep, rough, guttural voice that Nick remembered from his first encounter, the alien laughed and said "And you're the thing I am looking at." Nick studied the alien closely.

All of the facial features were in the same locations as a human's face. The alien's skin texture was rough like he imagined alligator skin would be. The skin color was a bluish-gray. His ears were similar to human ears but much narrower, longer, and flattened against the creature's head. The alien's nose, which was also narrower than a human's, almost had a point on it. The pupils of his eyes had a slight green glow that made Nick think of plastic toys that glowed in the dark. He had a strong jawline. His lips were also similar in color to a human's lips, only with a paler shade of red. When the alien had laughed, Nick saw a mouth full of pointed, conical teeth. The alien was void of hair, but his skin was darker and even rougher on the top of his head.

"Who are you?" Nick asked. The alien just laughed tauntingly as he walked back to the cab of the vehicle, leaving Nick's question unanswered. "So, even aliens can be jerks!" Nick yelled as the alien closed the door behind him.

* * * * *

They had been traveling for over two days when the man handcuffed Amber to the railing of the cushioned bench. The vehicle had accelerated to a much faster speed than Amber had believed the large vehicle could go. They were forced to slow down many times due to wreckage and road destruction, but after they would clear it, their high speed would resume. For the duration of the two days, they had only stopped to use the bathroom a few times. Amber had been trying to get some answers from the man, but he acted as though he didn't know what was going on himself. He was nervous and fidgety. With the new conditions, the handcuffs, and the accelerated speed, Amber was even more determined to find out some answers.

"Why do I have to be handcuffed?" Amber asked. "It's just routine, don't be offended." said the man. Amber knew he was lying. "Why did we start going so much faster?" she asked. "We're behind schedule." the man said. "What kind of schedule?" Amber asked. "I'm not in charge, I don't know." the man said firmly. "Why does the man in front always wear a helmet?" she asked. The man shifted uncomfortably. "Just protocol." he said. "Is this the military?" she asked. "No. Now please stop asking questions." he said. "Where are you taking me? Who are you?" Amber demanded with a frightened shakiness in her voice. "I'm just a regular person, like you!" he shouted. The man put his face in his hands and Amber could tell he was struggling to keep from crying. She was very surprised. The vehicle slowed and came to a stop. The door between the cab and the rear of the vehicle opened. The helmeted, suited figure was waiting for the man. The man raised his head from out of his hands and slowly stood up. He walked to the cab of the vehicle, and the door closed behind him. A few minutes later, he came back and sat down. The door closed and the vehicle began moving again. The man had much more composure than before, but he had a new look about him. He was no longer nervous and fidgety. Amber thought that she could see a cold hatred in his eyes. She did not feel as if it was for her, but she had a good idea who it was for, but she didn't quite understand why. "I didn't get you in trouble or anything, did I?" Amber asked quietly. The man looked at Amber as if he were looking at a small puppy that needed help. He shook his head no. He extended his first finger and pursed his lips against it, signaling Amber to remain quiet. He then mouthed the words *We'll talk later*. Amber nodded her head with understanding.

* * * * *

Keith opened his eyes to find himself inside of what appeared to be a science lab of some kind. When the science lab slowed, and then came to a complete stop, he discovered that he was half-right. It was some sort of science vehicle. He saw two men wearing white suits sitting across from him on a cushioned bench. Keith ascertained that he was lying on a cushioned bench as well, only he could not move. He had been handcuffed to the rails of the bench. From his vantage point, he noticed that both his backpack and his BB gun were stored on some racks along with other equipment that he did not recognize toward the back of the area in which he was laying. Keith assumed that he was in the large, white vehicle that had captured him. Almost everything around him was a clean, bright white. He supposed that the only germs in here were on him. The two men stood up. Before Keith could say anything, one of the men spoke. "You want to go?" he asked Keith. "Go where?" Keith asked hesitantly. "To the bathroom." the man said. "Uhh, yeah." said Keith. "Listen, go quick, and don't try anything. We've got to move fast." the man said as he removed the handcuffs from Keith. "Okay." said Keith. The man that had not spoken put on his helmet, and went out the door and down the ladder first. The other man motioned for Keith to go next. After he had put his helmet on, he followed Keith.

The place that they had stopped was in worse shape than Colfax had been. The buildings were crumbled. There were black streaks all over everything, where there had been multiple fires. The two men walked a few feet away from the vehicle and began doing their business. Keith stood next to the vehicle, waiting for them to finish. When they did, they walked back to the vehicle. "You done?" one of the men asked Keith. "No." he answered as he walked a short distance away from the vehicle. Keith took a stance and then looked back at the men. "I can't go if you're watching." he said. Keith heard the two men mumble as they turned and faced the vehicle. Keith quietly sprinted toward some of the ruined buildings. He clambered over a twisted pile of concrete debris and through what was left of a window of the second-closest building. He knew he would not have time to make it any further. He maneuvered carefully through the inside of the building. The only source of light was coming from the window he had climbed through. He found a large desk smashed up against one of the walls. He had to inhale to squeeze in behind it. He crouched down and got as comfortable as he could.

"Are you about done?" asked one of the men. There was no answer. The two men turned around. "Dang it, kid!" exclaimed one of them. They both jogged in the direction of the ruined buildings. It was the only place there was to hide. One man took the first building, and the other took the next.

"Hey, kid!" exclaimed the man as he carefully maneuvered over the same pile of concrete debris Keith had climbed only moments earlier. "Come on, kid, don't make this hard on yourself." he said as he ducked through the window. The man walked over to an over-turned table and lifted it up. He then began sifting through a small, lightweight pile of fragments. "Come on, kid, you don't want to anger them." he said as he continued his search. "It's starting to get dark." said the man. The man spotted the smashed-up desk. "It's no use, we're going to find you." he said as he approached the desk. He got a good grip on its edges and pulled hard. The desk crashed over on its side. The man found Keith crouched against the wall, holding his knees against his chest. The man could see the fright in Keith's eyes.

12

Interception

The preacher had found no survivors in Shreveport and had decided to continue north. During his three-day trip, he had collected some supplies. He had found himself a new pistol and plenty of ammunition. Although he had many models to choose from in the gun store, he chose to remain with a .38 like the one he already had. With all of the boxes of ammunition to put his mind at ease with this crazy world, John's mood began to change to one of calmness and serenity. He justified his acquisition of such large quantities of ammunition to himself with the acclamation "God needs me to protect the innocent!" Such was the methodology of his split-personality. In his mind, all of the events of atrocity and wrongfulness were completely misconstrued. The church, which had been full of God-fearing Christians, was locked up to protect them from the destruction that had been going on outside. The killings he had committed at the white vehicle were all self-defense. When John was in his personality of serenity and goodness, he could do no wrong. But once he crossed over to the darker reaches of his mind, a delicate balance was met: He could do no right.

The preacher had just entered what was left of Jefferson City, Missouri, when he saw another white vehicle. It was approaching from the east of the city. John quickly pulled his pickup behind a building, remembering all of the violence that had taken place at the last meeting with one of those vehicles. Violence was the last thing that Preacher Briggs wished for. After all, currently, he was a man of God.

The white vehicle headed for the building that the preacher had parked behind. It came to a stop directly in front of the building. The door at the rear of the vehicle opened and a suited figure climbed down the ladder. "Hey, where are we? Where are you going?" Mandy shouted after him. She was not surprised when there was no response. Preacher Briggs had been watching around a corner at the back of the building when the white vehicle disappeared to the front of it. When he turned to go look around the other corner, he found that he was already being approached by a suited figure. "Who are you people?" John Briggs asked the suited figure. "Sir, come with me." said the suited figure as he grabbed the Preacher roughly by the arms. He pulled him along to the front of the building. When he began to try to force the preacher up the ladder, John began to resist with more enthusiasm. He did not want to get into the white vehicle. "Get in!" yelled the suited figure. John kept pulling away from him. "What's going on out there?" asked Mandy. Both she and Marty had stood up as far as they could, trying to see out within the field-of-view limits placed on them by their handcuffs. "He's got a preacher out there." said Marty. The suited figure punched Preacher Briggs in the face. Mandy flinched with shock. "He hit him!" she exclaimed. The Preacher and the suited figure began grappling with each other on the ground. "We've got to do something!" exclaimed Mandy. "What can *we* do?" asked Marty rhetorically as he sat back down on the cushioned bench. The struggle outside became quiet. Moments later, the suited figure appeared in the doorway struggling to half-carry, half-drag the preacher inside of the vehicle. The suited figure was missing his helmet, and both he and the preacher had bloody faces and disheveled hair. The suited figure dropped the preacher and began dragging him toward the front of the vehicle. Mandy motioned to Marty by extending her leg straight out and pointing at it. Marty's brow lowered in puzzlement. Sudden comprehension kicked in as he threw his leg out in front of the suited figure, who was walking backward, pulling the preacher. The suited figure fell straight back, length-wise alongside the bench in front of Mandy and Marty. She grabbed the suited figure by the material of his suit and began pulling him toward the bench with all her might. Marty followed her lead. She stretched as far as her handcuffs would allow from the bench, and jumped on top of his chest, knocking the breath out of him. She grabbed the clip at his side and fumbled through the keys. She tried the smallest key first. Although it was not entirely like a typical handcuff key, it was the correct one, and she was quickly freed from her restraints. She hurriedly handed the keys to Marty, who wasted no time un-cuffing himself. Mandy handcuffed the suited figure to the same railing she had been handcuffed to. The door to the cabin opened, and another suited figure stepped into the rear of the vehicle. Marty rushed him, slamming him against the door frame, knocking something from his hand. He grabbed Marty by the shirt and slammed him up against the vehicle wall. Mandy ran toward the suited figured. She was rewarded with a hard backhand to the face. She fell to the floor in searing pain. He and Marty circled each other slowly, like two animals. Marty's jaw dropped when he saw another suited figure appear from outside of the vehicle, in the doorway. The one that he had been fighting, let out a deep, eerie laugh. The figure in the doorway was carrying some sort of device identical to the one the other figure had been carrying. He raised the device and pointed it into the door and a bright yellow beam leaped from it.

* * * * *

They had made one last stop to eat and use the bathroom. Once they were outside, the man removed his helmet and introduced himself to Amber. He very quickly explained to Amber that they must stop the man that was driving the vehicle. Carl Medwin was 43 years old. He was tall and sturdy. It looked as though his hair had only just begun to prematurely show some gray and begin to thin out. He had a kind face, but Amber knew he could be angered. She had seen that earlier when he was called to the front of the vehicle.

He gave her a brief, rough plan. "There's no time for any detailed explanation. When we stop again, we will be meeting another one of these vehicles. You're just going to have to trust me." said Carl. Amber tried to get more information from him, but he would say nothing more. He quickly led her back to the white vehicle. They traveled for several more hours before they again came to a stop, this time, in Jefferson City, Missouri. Carl unlocked Amber's handcuffs, put his helmet on, looked back and nodded, then went through the door and descended the ladder outside of the white vehicle. Amber began counting in a whisper.

* * * * *

Marty was so surprised that he couldn't speak. The beam of light hit the suited figure that he had been fighting. The body went limp and fell to the floor. Mandy was also momentarily at a loss for words. The other suited figure quickly stepped into the vehicle as he removed his helmet. "Don't be alarmed. There's no time to explain. We must work quickly." said the man. The man was Carl Medwin.

* * * * *

". . .23. . .24. . .25. . .26. . .27. . .28. . .29. . .30." Amber finished counting. She began yelling as if in fear just as Carl had instructed her to. The door between the front and rear of the vehicle opened, and a helmeted, suited figure rushed through the doorway. The suited figure looked closely at Amber and then began looking around, to see if he could find the source of her of her fear. "Hey." Amber said. He looked back at her. Amber fired the weapon that Carl had given her. A blinding beam of yellow light hit him. The suited figure slumped to the floor, and then was motionless.

* * * * *

"Listen! I hear someone screaming!" exclaimed Mandy as she almost lost her balance when Carl had begun to drive the white vehicle. He headed toward the other vehicle he and Amber had arrived in. He pulled up next to it and jumped out through the doorway. He quickly climbed the ladder and rushed through the doorway into the vehicle that Amber was in. He stopped dead in his tracks. Amber had the weapon pointed at him. She was shaking nervously. She had removed the helmet of the suited figure she had shot with the weapon. Even unconscious, the blue-grey alien seemed to grin in defiance through a mouthful of razor-sharp, conical teeth. "Amber, It's me, Carl." he said soothingly. She slowly lowered her weapon. Carl hugged her. "I know how you feel and I'll explain later, but we've got to move *now*. There's another vehicle out there with some people in it. Go get in it and tell them I'll be right there." he said, as he helped her through the door and onto the ladder. Carl began dragging the alien's body from the vehicle. When he got it out, he went into the other vehicle where Amber, Mandy, and Marty waited and the preacher lay unconscious. "Give me a hand." Carl said to Marty as he picked up the feet of the suited figure he had shot. "Everyone, please come outside." he said as he and Marty precariously carried the body down the ladder. Marty stared in horror at the alien they had placed next to the other suited figure. When everyone was outside, Carl removed the helmet from the other figure. It was also an alien. While the group of people looked closer at the aliens, he went around to the back of the abandoned vehicle and brought back a long, slender axe. It looked like a bush axe that a land surveyor would use, only it was one piece, made from some unknown alloy. Everyone flinched when Carl sliced open the first alien's chest. He searched around in it and found what he was looking for. The alien's heart was in approximately the same relative location as a human's heart. It was shaped somewhat differently and was completely bilateral in symmetry. Carl swung the axe and delivered several precise cuts, leaving the alien's heart lying in pieces. He opened the other alien's chest in the same location. "Let's hope they die just like we do." he said to the group. "Listen, I know that was very graphic and revolting to see, but you wouldn't believe the atrocities I have witnessed. We'll talk more about it when we have time." Carl added.

"Anyone have a lighter or some matches?" he asked. Mandy handed him her matchbook from the pocketbook she had recovered. He walked inside the other vehicle they were abandoning. When he came back out, smoke billowed up behind him. "Come quickly." he said as he climbed the ladder to the other vehicle. The group filed in behind him.

Carl was in the cab of the vehicle. There were two seats, and Amber joined him. "I'm glad you're here, Amber. I'm going to let you drive while I tell everyone what I know. The steering wheel is the same as any car steering wheel, as you can see. The acceleration is controlled by this throttle." he said, pointing to a large handle that looked like a gear shift. "The further you push the throttle forward, the faster we go. To stop, simply pull the throttle back to the middle. Be sure to move it slowly, because it will accelerate and decelerate accordingly. It's kind of like a boat with instantaneous response, understand?" asked Carl. "Yes, I got it." she said. She slowly pushed the throttle forward, and the white vehicle began to move. "Where're we going?" she asked. "I know that one of their main bases is up north, in Michigan. It's right at the coast of Keweenaw Point.

We'll head south. Just head out of this town and find the nearest interstate going south." he said. "Okay, I'll let you know if I have any problems." said Amber. "Good. I'm going to step into the back, but we'll be able to hear each other." Amber nodded.

Mandy was washing the blood from the preacher's face. He had regained consciousness but still seemed to be in a daze. All of the group had settled down on the long, comfortable, cushioned benches. The suited man that had been riding with Mandy and Marty was still handcuffed. He was sitting on the floor, at the end of the bench, closest to the back of the vehicle. Marty was leaning back comfortably, with his feet propped up. Carl walked to the back of the vehicle next to the handcuffed man and began speaking to the group.

"My name is Carl Medwin. I have been a traitor to you and perhaps to the entire human race. So has this man." Carl said pointing to the man on the floor. "The situation is very complex and there is much I do not know, but I will tell you what I do. If you haven't already come to terms with it, the creatures that you saw are aliens. I don't know where they have come from. Perhaps another galaxy. As far as I know, the planet Earth has been taken over and almost the entire population has been eradicated." he said. Mandy and Marty looked at each other with wide eyes. Carl continued. "The mass destruction is, of course, also their doing. Before it happened, many humans and their families were taken. We were scared into subservience by the threat of harm to our families if we did not comply. But we were given the promise of being reunited and allowed to live out the remainder of our lives with our families if we did comply. The mission of the group I'm in was a simple one. We had to go around the United States and collect the survivors. There are other units performing this same task in other countries. Your survival was not accidental. I don't know how or why, but they were able to spare your lives from the massive destruction. They are able to track you within a few feet, anywhere. I'm not very confident that we'll be able to escape them. I had a tough time making the decision I did. They probably would have killed my family anyway, but now they definitely will. I no longer think I could live with myself if I traded away innocent lives." said Carl. He paused a few moments to let the group think about what he had said. He then asked "Does anyone have any questions?" The group was silent.

13

Missouri Loves Company

The white vehicle that Carl had set on fire was now barely smoldering when another white vehicle approached from the west. It stopped near the smoking wreckage. Both doors opened at the same time and a suited figure hurried out of each of them. When the figures had reached the burned vehicle and had spotted the lifeless alien bodies, the one that had come from the cab ordered the others to get into the rear of the vehicle. The suited alien stood outside, pulled his helmet off, and threw it. He began yelling in a rage and hitting his fists onto the side of the burned vehicle.

"What's our short, blue friend so upset about?" Nick asked one of the suited men, expecting no reply. The skinny, suited black man glanced out the door to see that the alien was still rampaging around in anger. He then looked at the other man in expectation. The short, stocky man shrugged his shoulders. The black man said "Someone killed two of them." Nick's face lit up. "No kidding? Great! But, exactly, *who* are they?" asked Nick. "You'd better hope that Strax works out all of his anger before he sees you again."

said the short man. "So that's his name? Strax? Who is he?" Nick pressed. "They're aliens." said the black man. Nick looked down at the floor, thinking. Although Nick had already deducted that the strange-looking creature was an alien of some kind, he was dumbfounded to hear it said so bluntly. For a few moments, he felt as if he was watching everything that was going on from a distance as if he was watching a movie or having a nightmare. Nick looked back up at the black man. "Why do you follow his orders? I'd rather die than take orders from an alien!" said Nick. "I would too, but I'm not going to sacrifice my family." said the black man. Nick began to start understanding what was going on. "Oh, man, they have your family?" said Nick. "Yeah, that's why we don't dare try to escape or disobey." said the short man. "You know they're going to kill them anyway, don't you?" said Nick. "Shhh. Say no more." said the black man. The alien had returned. The vehicle began moving again. The white vehicle's antennae extended to their full lengths and Nick could hear the alien yelling something from the cab of the vehicle in his strange language.

* * * * *

The suited figure reached down and grabbed Keith's arm and began to pull Keith to a standing position. Keith was startled when a loud voice boomed out from the suited figure. "Report back. We will return for the boy. We have to continue immediately." a guttural voice came from the suited figure's helmet with a stream of radio static. "We're on our way." said the suited figure as he released Keith from his grip. The man removed his helmet. "Kid, you've got the luck of the Irish. Listen to me, now. If you see another one of these white vehicles, avoid it and run for your life. Somehow or another, they have the capability of tracking you. Good luck, kid." said the man as he replaced his helmet. The man left the building. Keith waited a few moments and then cautiously peered out a window. He watched the two figures climb the ladder into the back of the white vehicle. The vehicle began pulling away. *Who are they?* Keith wondered.

Inside the cab of the vehicle, a computer screen with a green dot and a flashing red dot went blank. It relit to a street atlas of the middle portion of the United States. There were six green dots on the screen. Four of them were moving and two of them were stationary but flashing. A blue line came from the green dot that represented the vehicle Keith had been traveling in and traced the shortest route from itself to the green dot that was moving the furthest south. The vehicle would follow that route.

As the vehicle pulled out from Keith's view from the window, he carefully walked out to the road. The sun had begun to go down, and Keith could see the headlights on the vehicle. He watched the lights get smaller and smaller as the vehicle accelerated down the road. The vehicle turned and went down an onramp onto an interstate highway. Keith watched it until it disappeared from his view. He began walking toward the highway.

* * * * *

Tracey noticed the sudden shift in direction and acceleration of the white vehicle. She didn't much care about it, though. She had been treated worse than she had ever been treated in her life. Her wrist was sore from the long hours of being handcuffed to the bench. Her face was a mess from her makeup, where she had been crying. She was irritable from the infrequent bathroom stops. Tracey had been riding for over three days. She wanted to take a hot bath. She wanted some real food, not the paste-crap they had been feeding her. She wanted everything to be the way it had been. On the few bathroom stops they had made, Tracey would again be forced to accept the fact that her days of glamour were over. As she absorbed her surroundings, the broken and crumbling buildings, the wrecked cars, and the ongoing silence, her mind played tricks on her, as she tried to picture herself in a science fiction movie.

Gradually, she began to get a grip on reality. She was no longer an actress, but an ordinary, helpless woman, who was beginning to give up hope of ever having any kind of life again.

* * * * *

The sudden outburst from the communication center in the cab of the white vehicle startled Amber. The white vehicle swerved slightly, but she quickly regained control. Carl Medwin and Mandy Richards entered the cab. "Dodge another pile of wreckage?" Carl asked. "No, the radio scared me." Amber said. The radio boomed out again in strange guttural sounds. "Is it them?" Mandy asked. "Yep, that's them. From the tone of voice, sounds like they might have found our little mess back in Jefferson City. My guess is that they're alerting the other collectors." said Carl. "How do you work that thing?" Amber asked. Carl examined the communications device. Although it was an alien device, like everything else in the white vehicle, its controls were not very different from any type of ham radio, CB, or other similar communications devices he had ever seen. The hand-held microphone/transmitter was wireless from the base unit. It looked very similar to a CB. "I think you just push this button." Carl said as he handed the hand-held attachment to Amber, tapping the button on the side. "Breaker, breaker you ugly aliens. You can just kiss our butts!" yelled Amber into the hand-held device. While Carl and Mandy were laughing at Amber's remark, the speaker on the base unit popped with static as a response came in. The same guttural voice that had sent the first transmission came from the communication center. The response was low in volume, and the words were carefully pronounced in perfect English. "You might had better kiss your own. Kiss them goodbye." said the alien transmission. Carl and Mandy stopped laughing. The three of them became silent. Amber slowly pushed the vehicle's power lever forward and it accelerated to an even higher rate of speed.

* * * * *

Keith had finally found what he had been looking for. A car that was undamaged, relatively small, keys were in the ignition, and it had an automatic transmission. The car was parked on the side of the road, along with the many other cars that were scattered around during the devastation. He had never driven a car before in his life, but he had driven a go-cart. *It's bigger and faster. How much different could it be?* Keith thought. Once behind the wheel, he closed the door and fastened his seat belt. He adjusted the seat and moved it as far forward as it would go. He made sure the shift lever was in the park position. He turned the key and pressed down on the accelerator. The engine roared to life. He pumped the gas pedal a few times. The engine revved like a tiger in the small sports car. He pulled the steering wheel to the right and held it. He pulled the lever to the drive position and pushed down on the gas pedal. The sports car leaped forward. The left-rear wheel dug a trench into the ground where it had been off of the pavement. The right-rear wheel squalled on the asphalt. Keith's head went back hard against the seat's headrest. The car went in a circle and came back around toward its original position. Before Keith could apply the brake, it bumped into the side of another car that had been behind it only a few moments earlier. Keith's body lurched forward, but the seatbelt held him firmly. He had released the gas pedal when he felt the sudden acceleration, but the momentum had already taken him around before he could think to press the brake pedal. Keith was exasperated and quickly switched the sports car off. He calmed down and began to breathe normally. He let his heart-rate slow back down. After a few minutes, he tried again. He kept his foot on the brake as he shifted into reverse. He slowly released the brake and slightly pushed the gas in. The car rolled back. Keith turned the steering wheel and shifted into drive. He slowly pushed the gas pedal down. When he felt as if he was accelerating too quickly, he would pull his foot completely off of the gas pedal. He carefully headed toward the onramp and then down the highway. He pulled the knob for the headlights and was relieved when they came on. Keith gradually became more familiar with driving the car and he would increase his speed as he became more comfortable. He would randomly slow back down to get a feel for the car's brakes. Gradually, he began to feel more confident in his ability to drive the sports car.

* * * * *

"We're leaving Missouri and entering Arkansas now." Amber said loudly so that everyone could hear. She had just driven by a welcome sign that had been spared from destruction. Carl entered the cab. "You get some rest now, I'll drive for a while." he said. "I'm okay." said Amber. "Come on, now. I'm sure you're fine, but you need to get rested up just in case." he said firmly as he put his hand on Amber's shoulder. "Alright." she said. Carl stood to the side and held the steering wheel. Amber quickly moved out of the seat and Carl quickly sat down, holding the steering wheel of the speeding vehicle steady. Amber walked to the rear of the vehicle.

As Amber walked back between the benches, someone grabbed her around the ankle. She screamed. The suited man that was hand-cuffed to one of the benches pulled her toward him. "Listen! We've got to turn back! Give ourselves up, before it's too late! You don't know what they'll do to you!" yelled the man. Mandy jumped up and pulled Amber away from the man. Preacher Briggs opened his sleepy eyes and looked around in confusion. Marty jumped up, as if ready to run. "What happened?" yelled Carl from the cab of the vehicle. "Everything's okay. This guy was just trying to scare every-one." responded Mandy. "We're all going to wish we were dead!" he yelled. The vehicle slowed to a stop. Carl left the cab and entered the back of the vehicle. As he walked by one of the exit doors, he pressed a button, and it hissed open. He uncuffed the man from the cushioned bench. Carl pulled the man up to his feet and dragged him to the door. "You want to turn back and give up?" Asked Carl.

The man responded, "If we don't listen to them, we're all going to die . . ." Carl said "I guess so." as he shoved the man out the door. He pushed the button to the door and it hissed shut. "Any objections?" Carl asked. There were no objections. Carl went back to the cab of the vehicle and it began to move once again.

14

Pursuits

"Where are we?" Nick asked as he felt the vehicle slow to a stop. "I don't know." said the black man. Nick heard the sound of a door hissing open from the front of the vehicle. "Our blue friend is gettin' out. How come none of us are?" Nick asked. "I don't know that either." said the black man. "Aren't you curious?" asked Nick. "Not enough to risk my family." said the black man. "Your family is as good as dead, anyway!" exclaimed Nick. The red-headed, red-bearded man jumped up from his bench and grabbed Nick around the neck. "You piece of garbage!" he said as he began choking Nick. The black man stood up and pulled him off of Nick. "Easy." said the black man. Nick began coughing from the strain his neck and windpipe had been under. "You alright, fella?" asked the black man. Through his coughing, Nick said "Yeah ... thanks." The red-headed man offered no apology. "Listen ... Mister ..." the black man said, pausing, as he invited Nick to tell him his name. "Call me Nick." he said. "Listen, Nick, I'm Brian. You could absolutely be right, but you're suggesting that we gamble with our families' lives." he said.

"Meanwhile, you're going around adding more innocent lives to the pot!" exclaimed Nick. He was silent for a few moments. "I'm going to see if Strax needs any help." he said, wanting to get away from Nick's convictions. "Our signal light's not on." said the red-headed man. Brian was not paying any attention to his white-suited associate. He pressed a button and the vehicle's rear door hissed open.

* * * * *

The sports car rolled along smoothly under the control of first-time automobile driver Keith Westman. Although there was wreckage and debris everywhere, Keith had very little trouble getting through. The white vehicle's wonderful snowplow-type blade kept a clean, clear path in front of him. He had spotted the vehicle a few times far off in the distance, whenever there was a long line of sight ahead. He was very thankful his father had taught him how to siphon because he found that the car was running low on gas. He managed to find some slim piping in a work truck on the side of the road. He tried siphoning gas from a few of the newer cars and didn't have any luck. He finally found an old model flatbed truck to get the gas from. He seemed to remember that his father had said something about the difficulties of siphoning from newer cars.

Keith desperately wanted to continue his pursuit, but by morning, he could hardly keep his eyes open. He began drifting to sleep and causing the car to weave back and forth. He almost went off of the road a few times. He finally stopped at the remains of a store. He parked the car and tiredly dragged his feet into the broken building. Keith found himself a safe, cool, and comfortable spot beside a collapsed aisle of canned goods. He curled up and went to sleep.

* * * * *

"Here." said the female suited figure as she offered Tracey a tube of food paste. Tracey turned away without speaking. "Well, don't whine about being hungry later." she snapped. The suited female figure and her male counterpart ate their paste in silence.

* * * * *

"How long have you been here?" the suited figure asked in a deep, guttural voice. The man that Carl had pushed out was on his knees, sobbing in front of the suited figure who was asking the questions. "Only a little while. They wouldn't listen to me! I tried to stop them, you've got to believe me!" sobbed the man as he lowered his head down to one of Strax's boots and cried on it. Strax pulled his foot away with revulsion. As he raised his weapon, the rear door of the vehicle hissed open. Brian had opened the door just in time to see Strax fire the energy weapon at the man kneeling and sobbing in front of him. The man screamed with intense pain. There was a crackling sound similar to that of pine knots exploding in a fireplace. The man turned red and disappeared in a shower of sparks. Brian shuddered when Strax looked up and stared back at him. "Uh-oh." Brian said.

* * * * *

Keith had only slept for a few hours. He felt like sleeping the whole day, but he couldn't get the pursuit of the vehicle off of his mind. He made a quick meal of a peanut butter sandwich and some potato chips. Even though the store's cooler was indeed still cool, he thought twice and decided not to eat anything from it. He wondered how long it would be until the stench of rotten food would be rising from buildings all throughout the United States. *And maybe the world.* Keith shuddered at the thought. He washed his meal down with a cool drink, and then gathered some supplies. He quickly put a few armfuls of food, flashlights, batteries, and other items he felt would be useful into the back seat of the sports car. He figured that he would probably not have a problem finding more supplies, but it was better to be safe than sorry. He started up the car and continued down the road.

15

Never Too Late to Change

Brian quickly pressed the button again and the rear door of the vehicle hissed as it closed back. "He just killed one of us. Are you with me or not?" Brian asked, hastily directing the question to his suited partner. The red-headed man was in shock at Brian's question. "Are you nuts? He'll kill you too. I'm not going against Strax." answered the man. Brian raised his weapon and fired on his partner. When the yellow beam hit the man, he slumped over, unconscious. Brian opened the door that separated the rear of the vehicle from the cab and went in. "Hey, what about me?" yelled Nick from the bench he was handcuffed to. "No time!" yelled Brian as the vehicle lurched backward. After a few seconds, the vehicle suddenly jerked, lurched forward, and accelerated at a remarkable rate. Nick heard a loud thud up against the vehicle. "Take this, you lyin' scumbag!" yelled Brian as he hit Strax with the white vehicle.

* * * * *

The white vehicle that Tracey was in slowed to a stop where there was a suited figure lying in the middle of the road. Two others got out of the back of the white vehicle. One suited figure got out of the front cab. They all approached the suited figure lying on the road. The one from the cab knelt down and rolled the body over. Strax slowly opened his eyes. He grunted as he got up and began yelling in his strange, guttural language. The one from the cab of the vehicle snapped back at Strax in the same tone. Strax stopped yelling. "Let's go," said the one from the cab to the two figures that were waiting behind him. He and Strax got into the cab of the vehicle and the other two got into the back.

* * * * *

Carl stopped at a convenience store, at the top of an offramp, only a few hundred feet from the interstate. "Let's eat, stretch, and take care of business quickly. I have no way of knowing if we're being followed yet, and if so, how far away they are." he said after everyone had left the vehicle. They all carefully entered the cracked building.

The store was thankfully devoid of any dead bodies. There were only a few collapsed display stands to show that anything was even wrong with the inside of the building. They took turns using the store's bathroom. Afterward, they began to quickly browse for their meals. "Don't get anything from the refrigerator, it looks as if the food has begun to spoil." Preacher Briggs warned the group. He was now in a peaceful, kind mood. "Anybody want chips?" asked Mandy. "I do," said Amber. Amber joined Mandy at the chips display. Carl had opened a box of trash bags and was filling them with supplies. Marty was doing the same. After they had collected all they wanted, they went back outside. Carl and Marty loaded the bags into the white vehicle and then joined Amber and Mandy where they had sat down on the curb to eat.

"Carl, we haven't really had a chance to thank you for what you've done. The sacrifices you might have made." said Mandy as she wiped some crumbs from her mouth. "There's no need. We're all in this together." he said. "Have you thought about where we're going?" Mandy asked. Carl sighed. "Yes, I have. As I said before, I think it's just a matter of time before they catch us, but I think our best chance is the ocean." he said. "What exactly do you mean?" asked Mandy. "A boat!" exclaimed Amber when she caught on to what Carl was leading up to. "Right!" Carl exclaimed with the same enthusiasm Amber had let shine through. "Oh, great. We're going to get on a boat and die out on the ocean, instead of at the hands of aliens." said Marty. Mandy looked at Marty scornfully. Marty shrugged. "No, not at all. I figured that we can find a big boat, or even a yacht, fill it with supplies - especially fishing supplies and water - and stay off of the coast as much as possible. We sneak back whenever we need more water or supplies. These white vehicles are fancy, but I really don't think that our blue friends have planned for this contingency." explained Carl. "What about their ability to track us? And these things are aliens, they obviously will have other vehicles in which to pursue us. Or they could just get a boat, too, Einstein." Said Marty. "Why are you so rude?" Mandy snapped at Marty rhetorically. Preacher Briggs put a gentle hand on Marty's shoulder. "Give him a chance, Marty." said the Preacher. "It's alright. He has good points. The truth is, I *don't* know the answers and I *don't* know what's best. It just seems that pursuing us on water would maybe make us a little more trouble than we're worth to them." said Carl. "I agree." said Amber. "I can't think of anything better. I think what Carl proposes is reasonable." said Preacher Briggs. "Me too. What about you, *Einstein?*" said Mandy as she turned toward Marty. "I guess so. I just wish we knew how they were tracking us." Marty said. "Well, let's think about it." said Mandy. Amber turned her cola up to finish it off. Her eyes widened and she slowly stood up. "You already figured it out?" asked Mandy. Amber quickly shook her head. "No? Then what's wrong?" Mandy asked. Amber pointed down the long stretch of cracked interstate they had been traveling. They all turned their heads to look. They saw not only one white vehicle, but a second one was speeding not far behind the first one. "Let's go!" Carl yelled. Mandy grabbed Amber by the wrist and pulled her toward the vehicle. The sudden jolt broke her paralysis. Marty had needed no stimulus. He was the first one in the vehicle. Preacher Briggs waited to make sure everyone got in and then followed.

Carl hesitated before he started the vehicle into motion. "What's wrong?" asked Amber, who was sitting in the seat beside him. "We'll never outrun them, even if we don't get back on the highway. It looks like it won't be much longer until they catch us. I hadn't realized they had been closing in on us so fast. The other collectors must have been dispatched at the same time as we were, to the area where we met Mandy and Marty." said Carl, solemnly. "Well, let's get moving. Maybe we've got enough time to find a place to at least make a stand." said Mandy from the open doorway, between the cab and the rear of the vehicle. "We won't find good cover on the highway." said Marty from the back of the vehicle. "No, we won't. Let's just head down this road." said Carl as he pushed the acceleration lever forward. The tires boiled smoke and the tracks left ruts in the asphalt from the sudden acceleration. Mandy held on tightly to the doorjamb between the cab and the rear.

* * * * *

In the rearview monitor, Brian saw a vehicle gaining on Nick and himself. When he looked back up, through the windshield, he briefly caught a glimpse of another white vehicle at the top of the upcoming onramp. He had no way of knowing that the vehicle in front of them was driven by a man named Carl Medwin and had all human passengers. The vehicle had disappeared, but the smoke that had boiled out from under its tires and tracks was still settling. "We got one behind us, and one in front of us, man!" Brian yelled back to Nick. "Let me loose!" yelled Nick. "If I stop, they're gonna catch us!" replied Brian. Brian expected the other vehicle to head down the onramp and try to head him off. After a few seconds had passed, and he didn't see the other vehicle, he decided to take the offramp and head toward where it had just been. *They must have gone down the other side, assuming that I was not going to take the offramp.* he thought. When he got to the top of the offramp, he still did not see the other vehicle. Thinking that the other vehicle had went down the ramp toward the interstate, Brian turned right. The pursuing vehicle was only a few hundred yards behind them. As the road straightened out, Brian pushed the lever forward as far as he dared.

* * * * *

They were halfway across a bridge when Carl yanked the lever back to the middle position. The vehicle skidded sideways with loud squealing from the tires and heavy scrapes from the lightweight tracks. The other side of the bridge was gone. It had collapsed into the water below. He began maneuvering the vehicle so as to get it turned around. Before he could get it even turned part-way, he looked up to see two vehicles speeding right toward them. They looked like they were going much too fast to stop in time. Carl had no maneuvering room to get the vehicle turned around at the end of the bridge. "Everyone, out! Now!" he yelled as he smacked the button that opened the cabin door. Mandy opened the rear door and everyone filed out as fast as they could. Marty was, of course, in the lead.

Brian had decided to ram the white vehicle that was blocking his path across the bridge. He made a shocking discovery when he was already too close to stop in time. Every person that he could see scrambling out of the vehicle in front of him seemed to be plain-clothed humans. "Those deviants! It looks like they're using innocent people to blockade us!" yelled Brian. As he pulled the lever back to attempt a stop, there was a flash of light. The vehicle behind him had fired a weapon. The two men felt the jolt of the weapon as it blasted against one of the tracks of the vehicle. The vehicle turned sideways and became airborne. It crashed down on its side, and began sliding toward the other vehicle at the end of the broken bridge. Sparks flashed around the vehicle as it slid. Nick had heard Brian yell for him to hang on. *Like I got a choice.* was Nick's last thought before they smashed into the other vehicle.

Everyone dove for cover, trying to get out of the way of the sliding vehicle. As it impacted, the vehicle that Carl had been driving was knocked off of the end of the bridge. There was a loud clash of metal and concrete as pieces of both vehicles flew into the air, along with pieces of the concrete side-railing of the bridge. There was a tremendous splash when the other vehicle hit the river. The vehicle that Brian, Nick, and the unconscious redheaded man were in, skidded to a halt and teetered dangerously on the broken edge of the end of the bridge. Metal, concrete, and dust whooshed down from the air. The pursuing vehicle screeched to a stop less than 100 yards from the end of the bridge and the vehicle that was delicately balanced on its side at the end of the bridge. Strax and his suited alien companion got out of the cab of the vehicle. The two humans in the back also got out, suited, with helmets. Strax was not wearing his helmet. All of them were carrying weapons. Strax laughed in his deep, guttural voice. The four of them began to walk toward the end of the bridge, the teetering vehicle, and the humans crouched in cover.

* * * * *

Nick was hanging sideways, strapped to the bench, looking down at the bloodied face of his new friend. "Are you okay?" Nick asked. "I'm in better shape than you'll be in if we fall into the river." said Brian. "Get me outta here! I feel this heap swaying!" exclaimed Nick. "Shhh. They're right outside." whispered Brian as he quickly removed the handcuffs that had Nick bound to the bench, and did his best to keep him from smacking down to the other side of the vehicle when he was free.

Nick was rubbing his sore wrists when Brian offered his hand. Nick looked at him questioningly. "Brian Stanton." Brian said, introducing himself. "Nick Tyler." replied Nick. Nick was quiet for a moment. "What's the situation?" Nick asked. "We just knocked one of these fancy rides into the river. There are innocent people out there. I guess we'll have alien company any minute now." said Brian. As if to confirm Brian's statement, they heard Strax's deep laugh. "Do we have any weapons?" Nick asked. "These." said Brian handing Nick one of the handheld weapons. Nick studied the weapon. He then pushed the door button. The door hissed open, scraping the pavement underneath. "Wait! What's your plan?" asked Brian. "Plan? I don't have a plan!" said Nick with a laugh. He pulled himself out the door of the laterally positioned vehicle and then began firing the weapon. "The man ain't right." said Brian as he ran out the door to join Nick's insane assault.

Nick had hit the alien beside Strax. The alien yowled in pain. The strange popping and crackling sound followed, and then the alien turned red and disappeared in a shower of sparks. Strax dropped to the ground and began firing instantly. Nick and Brian returned fire. Strax and one of the humans hit Nick. Thankfully for Nick, Strax had ordered them to have their weapons on the stun setting. Nick slumped over instantly. Brian managed to take out one of the humans before he was stunned unconscious. "Anyone else?" Strax asked the wide-eyed humans in his guttural tone. "Come forward!" Strax demanded. None of the humans moved. "Very well." said Strax as he and the remaining suited human began walking toward the group. "Mr. Medwin, your family and Mr. Stanton's family aren't going to be very appreciative of your disobedience. We would like to take the others alive, but you two . . . you two can die for leading us on such an inconvenient pursuit." said Strax as he adjusted his handheld weapon to the kill setting and then pointed it at Carl. The suited human beside Strax also set his handheld weapon to the kill setting and then pointed it at Brian, who lay unconscious. "You ugly space vermin!" said Carl, looking his enemy defiantly in the eyes. Strax began laughing. To everyone's surprise, between Strax, his suited human slave, and the group of humans, a pile of lightweight debris and rubble began to shift and rise up. From the wreckage arose Preacher John Briggs.

16

Guess Who's Coming for Sinners?

The Preacher arose with a sinister laugh that was eerily similar to the laugh that belonged to Strax. Strax was taken by surprise. "Come my child." said Briggs as he stepped forward and hugged Strax around the neck. Everyone could see the look of part-revulsion, part-puzzlement on the alien's face, over the preacher's shoulder. Strax could also see the puzzled looks that everyone else had. As the preacher embraced his enemy, another white vehicle pulled up beside the one Strax had arrived on. Strax heard the radio sound off in the human's helmet. It snapped him out of his perplexed state and he began to push the preacher away. The power of Preacher John Briggs' grip he had on Strax tremendously increased, and he yanked the alien's neck to one side. There were multiple pops as the alien's neck broke in several places. "Hallelujah!" exclaimed the preacher as he held onto the dead alien and twisted him around toward the suited human next to him. He pointed Strax's hand, which still held its weapon, toward the suited human. He pushed down on the alien's fingers, and the red beam hit the suited human. The human screamed, turned red, crackled, popped, and vanished in a shower of sparks. The humans cheered as Preacher Briggs pulled the hand-held weapon from the alien's hand, as he let Strax's lifeless body slump down onto the hard-top. John whirled around and looked at the cheering humans. He was puzzled. He slowly raised the weapon and pointed it at the group of humans. They stopped cheering. "Preacher, what are you doing?" Mandy asked. A red beam flashed by the Preacher's head. It struck the white vehicle at the end of the bridge. An area on the vehicle turned bright red, and then crackled, popped, and left a jagged, gaping hole in the vehicle. The vibration started the vehicle teetering once again. Preacher John Briggs spun around and faced three oncoming, suited assailants. He returned their fire. He killed one of them before they hit him. The Preacher slumped to the ground, unconscious. The other two continued to approach, constantly firing their weapons. Carl ran for the weapon that the Preacher had been using. He was hit, and dropped to the asphalt, unconscious. The remaining humans began to scramble for better cover, as the aliens had gotten to close to dare try for the preacher's weapon again. As the suited figures got even closer to the humans and the wreckage at the end of the bridge, they all heard the loud reverberations of a high RPM gasoline engine quickly approaching.

17

Good Thing, Small Package

The two suited figures whirled around to see a sports car coming down on them. Keith yanked the steering wheel to the left while applying the brakes and hit the two suited figures perfectly as if a baseball bat hitting a baseball for a home run. The car screeched to a stop only a few feet from where Carl and the Preacher lay unconscious. Keith jumped out of the car and ran around to the side where he had hit the two suited figures. He removed the first figure's mask. Keith's heart leaped when he saw a blue creature staring through him, with dead eyes. He cautiously walked backward, away from the alien. He stumbled and fell on top of the other suited figure. The figure grunted, and Keith hurriedly got back to his feet. He carefully removed the mask. It was the man that had let him go when he had tried to escape, during their bathroom stop. There was blood coming from his mouth and nose, but he was conscious. Keith knelt down beside him. "Kid, it's you." whispered the man. "I'm ... I'm sorry." said Keith as tears began to well up in his eyes. He had seen suited figures firing their weapons at people. He had to stop them, but he was still feeling the impact of what he had just done. "Shhhh, It's okay. It's the best thing that could have happened to me." whispered the man. "What do you mean?" asked Keith through his tears of guilt. The man weakly grasped Keith's hand. "It was one of the toughest decisions ..." the man said as he began coughing up blood. Mandy, Marty, and Amber, the remaining humans that were not unconscious, began to come out of the wreckage they had been using for cover. They approached Keith and the dying man. "... I know now it was the wrong one. Good luck, Kid ..." whispered the man. It was his the last thing he said.

* * * * *

Keith stood up. "Does anyone know what's going on?" he asked with a hoarse throat as he began to cry. Mandy hugged him. "You saved us. We'll all talk later, but let's not lose the time you've given us." she said as she comforted him. "Amber, go get one of those vehicles." said Mandy as she began to take charge. "Marty, let's you and I check on everyone that's down, and get them ready to go." she said as she released Keith from her embrace. "Are you okay?" He nodded and leaned against the car and put his hand over his eyes, and wiped the tears on his face. Mandy and Marty began to check all of the fallen humans.

* * * * *

Amber got the white vehicle as close to the wreckage as she could, and then stopped. When she got out, she called for Mandy. Amber opened the side door and pointed. Mandy climbed the ladder with Amber following her. "This is Tracey Blaine!" said Mandy. "That's who I thought it was, but I wasn't sure." said Amber. "Miss Blaine?" Mandy asked. Tracey was looking away, in a daze. "I think she's in shock or something." said Amber. "Yeah, me too. We'll get those handcuffs off of her when we get Carl into the vehicle. I know he's got some keys." said Mandy. "Is he and the others okay?" asked

Amber. "As far as we can tell, they're just unconscious." said Mandy. They left the vehicle and began loading all of the unconscious passengers inside.

* * * * *

"Marty, we're not going to leave without you!" Mandy exclaimed as Marty quickly pushed his way by others, up the ladder, into the vehicle "Is that everything and everyone?" Mandy asked aloud. "That kid didn't get in." said Amber. Mandy went back out of the vehicle. She saw Keith sitting in the car. "Would you like to come with us?" she asked. Keith was quiet for a moment. "Yeah, I figured I'd follow you." he said. "There's plenty of room if you want to ride with us." said Mandy. "I don't know." said Keith, hesitantly. He tried to think of a reason that made sense, only he couldn't. "I'm sorry, I just feel like I might need to be by myself right now. I can't really explain it." he said. "That's okay. We've all been through a lot. I can understand why you might want to be on your own and alone right now. It's gonna be hard to learn to trust again. We're eventually going to have to, now, more than ever, and then if we manage to get through this mess. You take whatever time you need, but know we're here if you need us." she said as she turned to walk back to the white vehicle. Keith was surprised that she didn't try to coax him into coming. "Wait." he said. He got out of the car and jogged up beside her. She hugged him around the shoulders as they walked and they continued to the vehicle.

* * * * *

"Let's go." Mandy said as the door closed. "Roger." Amber said from the cab. The vehicle moved backward and then turned around. They began to travel back down the road that had led them to the fallen bridge. Keith saw that they had carefully placed two unconscious men on the floor. One of them appeared to be a preacher, the other one was wearing the dreaded, white radiation-type suit. There was also a skinny black man wearing a white suit, securely strapped onto a cushioned bench on one side of the vehicle and an average-sized white man strapped onto the cushioned bench on the opposite side. There was a glamourous, red-haired woman sitting on one of the benches, staring at the floor. There was a man sitting opposite her with a nervous look on his face. Of course, it was Marty. "Why are those two men strapped down?" Keith asked. "Have a seat." said Mandy as she sat down on a cushioned bench. Keith sat down beside her. "My name is Mandy Richards." she said. "Keith Westman." said Keith. "That's Marty Maxx." she said. Marty nodded toward Keith. Keith nodded back. "That's Tracey Blaine, the actress, who hasn't spoken to anyone yet. On the floor are Preacher John Briggs and Carl Medwin. You'll have to introduce yourself to them later, I guess. We don't know who these two men are. They were among the ones in the gun fight, but we don't really know anything about them." she said pointing to Nick and Brian. "Our driver is Amber Kentwood." she said. "Amber, this is Keith Westman." she shouted to the front of the cab. "Nice to meet you." Amber shouted back. "Nice to meet you, too." shouted Keith. They were momentarily silent. "What can you tell me about what has happened?" Keith finally asked. "Well, I don't want to sugar-coat it, so I'll just be blunt. It seems that we are in the middle of an alien invasion." Mandy said. Keith was again silent. "I know it sounds unbelievable, but look at what's happened." said Mandy. "Why are *we* still alive and who are the humans in suits?" asked Keith. "The men in suits were sent around with some of the aliens to gather us up. We don't know why they want *us*, and if our survival was intentional or not." said Mandy. "Where are we going?" Keith asked. "South, to the ocean. We're going to get a boat and stay out to sea as long as we can, coming to shore only when we have to get supplies." said Mandy. Keith was silent for a moment before he spoke. "Do you think that will keep us safe? I figure aliens would be able to fly after us." said Keith. "You're right, Keith. We don't know really know what the best course of action is. We kind of figured that maybe fooling with us out in the water might be an irritation to them or an inconvenience. Maybe one where they would just leave us be. We have all discussed it, and it was all we could really think of in the short time we had. If you have any other ideas, we would sure listen to them. " said Mandy. Keith nodded as he thought about her answer.

* * * * *

A few hours later, the unconscious men began to awaken. The preacher was again in his docile state of pleasantness. He took a seat next to Mandy on the cushioned bench. "Are you okay, hero?" asked Mandy. "Me? A hero?" said the preacher. "Yes! You got three of them!" exclaimed Mandy. Preacher Briggs thought for a moment. "Oh, yes." said the preacher as he struggled to remember and understand what Mandy was talking about. "You're one tough customer for a preacher. I was a little worried when you turned toward us with that weapon, though. I thought you were going to shoot us! Then, you turned around and surprised the ones that had arrived! That was great." said Mandy. "Uh, thank you." he said, very confused. He had no earthly idea as to what Mandy was talking about. He just went along with it.

"I can't believe I'm alive." said Carl as he stood up. "Carl, are you okay?" Amber shouted from the front of the cab. "Yes, Amber, I'm fine, thank you." said Carl. "When I saw the preacher go down, I thought for sure we were going to get it. What happened after I was hit?" asked Carl. "The kid there." said Marty. "Out of nowhere, Keith came to our rescue." he added. "Yeah, smacked two of them with a car." said Mandy. Keith shifted uncomfortably in his seat. "How old are you, son?" asked Carl. "Fifteen." he said. "I guess we're all lucky that you know how to drive at such a young age." said Carl. "I've only known how for a few days." said Keith. "How did you manage to show up here just when we needed you most?" Carl asked. "I was captured, but I managed to escape. For whatever reason, they stopped trying to catch me and left. I followed them." said Keith. "Good going." said Carl, putting his hand on Keith's shoulder. "Thanks," said Keith. "What about these two? Why are they handcuffed?" Carl asked Mandy. "Yes, why, why, why are my poor wrists subjected to this torture once again by my own friendly human race?" snapped Nick. He had just awakened and was in a very cynical mood. Brian had awakened also. "They got my butt tied down too, Nick!" exclaimed Brian. Nick laughed hysterically. "I'd give you a high-five, Brian, but someone still has my darn hands cuffed to this stupid bench that I am very, very, tired of being strapped to!" exclaimed Nick as his voice got louder and louder. Carl removed Nick's handcuffs. "Thank you very much. Do I really look like a blue alien? I don't seem to be dressed in a white jump suit either, do I?" snapped Nick. Everyone was quiet, as they let Nick get his frustrations out of his system and calm down. After a few moments of silence, Nick said "I'm sorry ... it's been a rough ride. Brian put his butt on the line to save me. Evidently, like yourself, he's not a *bad guy* anymore." Carl removed Brian's handcuffs. "My name's Nick Tyler." offering his hand to Carl. They shook. "Carl Medwin." There were introductions all around for Brian and Nick. "This woman appears to be Tracey Blaine, the actress, but she hasn't talked to anyone." said Carl as he referred to the woman wearing the blue dress. "The young lady that is driving this vehicle is named Amber Kentwood." said Carl as he led Nick and Brian to the cab of the vehicle. "This is Nick." Amber glanced over at Nick, quickly, and then looked back at the highway. She extended one hand, while keeping the other on the steering wheel, and quickly shook his hand. "Nice to meet you." she said. "You too. Wow, you look a little young to be operating this big, fancy wonder of technology." said Nick. "I'm sixteen." she said, a little indignantly. "And she can probably drive it better than any of us!" Carl exclaimed. "Hey, no complaint here, it was merely a compliment." said Nick. Amber smiled. She gave Brian the same quick greeting and handshake. Carl, Brian, and Nick all walked back to the rear of the vehicle.

"So, where are we going?" Nick asked. Carl explained the plan of hiding out at sea to the newcomers, although Keith had already heard some of it from Mandy. Tracey was still not responsive to anyone's attempt to communicate. After Carl finished and a few moments of silence, Nick began to shake his head. "I have to disagree." he said. "Well, if you think you have a better idea, I'm sure we would all love to hear the details." said Carl. "Can't we stop somewhere and discuss this over something to eat and drink?" said Nick. "Sure, but can you just give me an idea of what your better plan is." said Carl. "It's not necessarily a *better* plan, but maybe just the better thing to do." said Nick.

18

The New Leader

Carl had instructed Amber to get off at the next exit. They were going to find a food store of some kind where they might rest, use the bathroom, and discuss possible courses of action concerning their predicament. Amber found a large grocery store that looked as if it had missed most of the destruction of that terrible day. She stopped the white vehicle right at the front entrance. Mandy tried to get Tracey to come with them, but she still wasn't talking. Everyone else got out and went shopping.

* * * * *

Carl was teamed up with Amber. They had begun to have a somewhat father-daughter type of relationship. Carl called to Keith who had been walking by himself. "Why don't you walk with us?" asked Carl. "Thanks." he said, as he joined them. "You kids should give some serious considerations to dating. There may be no one else." said Carl. Keith turned red with embarrassment. "Carl!" said Amber as she gently elbowed him. She looked over at Keith and she also felt her face flush as it turned red.

Marty was following Mandy around the store. Nick caught up to them. "So, what's a nice girl like you doing in a catastrophe like this?" Nick asked Mandy. "Nice girl? Yeah, I'm a nice girl." she said with sarcasm. "What do you mean by that?" he asked. "Nothing." She responded. "So, Nick, I wonder if your plan is any more foolish than Carl's?" Marty interrupted from behind. "I don't know, Marty. It *may be* more foolish." said Nick. "Carl's plan is not foolish." snapped Mandy. "Are you and Carl, you know, together?" asked Nick. "Together? Is this really a good time to be asking such questions?" asked Mandy. "I was just wondering..." Nick began. "Well, we're not together!" snapped Mandy. "I was just trying to make conversation." said Nick as he abruptly walked away from Mandy and Marty.

Brian and the preacher had talked together as they collected what they wanted from the grocery store. Brian got the things he liked. Preacher Briggs got the things that were good for him. "From what I've heard recounted from the group about your heroism, Preacher, you have definitely been taking your supplements." said Brian. He smiled at Brian as he wondered why everyone kept referring to him in a heroic manner.

* * * * *

There was a cool breeze blowing across the group of people that had seated themselves on the cool grass, in the shade, next to the large grocery store. The day was clear and the sun was very bright and hot, but the shade provided them protection from its rays. The area they had stopped in was rural, and there were only a few buildings scattered out across the beautiful landscape of whatever small town they were in. They were only a few miles from the interstate they had been traveling on, heading southward, down toward the Gulf of Mexico.

Everyone was quietly eating their meals when Nick stood up and slammed his sandwich down on the ground and jumped up and down on it, squishing it to mush. Everyone stopped eating and looked at Nick with concern. "Look out there! What do you see?" Nick yelled at the top of his lungs as he swept his arm around toward the beautiful countryside of the small town. The group was quiet. "Well? Anybody?" Nick yelled. "Land?" asked Brian. "What else?" Nick asked. "Trees." said Amber. "Yes, what else?" Nick asked. "Some buildings." said Marty. "Roads." said Keith. "The beautiful, blue sky." said Mandy. "That's right. All of those things. And whose are they?" Nick asked. "Nobody owns them now, I guess." said Brian. "I say someone does. I say we do! This is *our* planet!" yelled Nick. "They took our planet from us! I say we take it back!" yelled Nick. "Yeah!" yelled Keith. Everyone else remained quiet. Mandy finally spoke. "Do you know how crazy that sounds? Are you insane?" said Mandy. "As a matter of fact, somewhat clinically so! But not as crazy as my fellow Earthlings who are willing to put their tails between their legs and run away, whimpering!" snapped Nick. The group looked shocked and hurt at his remarks. "Nick, it's not that any one of us would be scared as you seem to be implying, but there's only nine of us. It would seem to be a futile effort." said Carl. "We've beat them so far." said Nick. "They didn't think there was going to be any resistance. They know better now. And the truth is, we probably got lucky most of the time." said Carl. "Yeah, there's no way we could win." said Marty nervously. Nick turned away from the group and sighed. In a whisper, Nick said "Winning's not the point. It's knowing in our hearts that we tried. Even if we all did die." Nick lowered his head. Surprisingly, Keith stood up and went to Nick's side. "They killed my parents." Keith said as he began to tear up. Preacher Briggs joined them. "They've killed nearly everybody. It is said by many that *God helps those who help themselves*. But the truth is that God also helps the helpless, just as the Good Book says in Isaiah 41:10 *Fear thou not; for I am with thee: be not dismayed; for I am thy God: I will strengthen thee; yea, I will help thee; yea, I will uphold thee with the right hand of my righteousness.* I'm with you, son." said the preacher. Amber looked at Carl questioningly. He nodded as if to tell her it was okay if she agreed with Nick. Amber stood next to Keith. "They killed my dad." she said as tears began to well up in her eyes. Keith put his hand on her shoulder. She pulled him to her and they embraced, both of them crying. "Deep down, I always thought that resistance was the right thing to do." said Brian as he stood up and put his hand on Nick's back in a friendly gesture. Nick turned around and looked at the three that remained sitting. He focused his attention on Mandy. Nick's eyes were now glistening with the tears he es holding back. "How could you ever enjoy looking at that beautiful, blue sky, knowing that it was no longer a symbol of freedom?" Nick said pleadingly as a tear slid down his face. Mandy stood up and went to him. She embraced him. "I didn't know how deeply you felt. I'm sorry if I misjudged you, Nick." said Mandy.

"Listen, everyone. I do understand how you all feel, but I've seen their base of operations! Their complex is massive! Their technology is superior! There's no way you can penetrate it! They also have the numbers! We will all die!" exclaimed Carl as he stood up. "Carl, I think you've missed the whole point! I've seen the complex too! It doesn't matter if we die!" snapped Brian. "I don't want to die! I say we take our chances on a boat!" yelled Marty. Several of the group began talking at the same time. Nick and Mandy released each other from their embrace. "Settle down, everyone, please!" Nick shouted. The group became quiet. "Let's go ahead and straighten this out. No one has to do anything they don't want to do. We'll go our separate ways, if you want." added Nick. "I don't think that will be necessary, Nick. There's no sense in separating. Majority rules. Although I do think our chances are better with the plan of going to the ocean, I had also dwelled upon the idea of fighting against them. I just want to make sure that everyone understands the risks involved if we do choose this course of action. No hard feelings?" said Carl as he extended his hand to Nick. They shook hands. "United we stand."

said Nick. "Divided we fall." said Carl. "You people are all crazy!" yelled Marty, beginning to panic. "You're going to get us all killed!" he added. "Marty, you don't have to go. You can stay wherever you wish. But you will be alone. Would you rather be alone?" asked Carl. Marty shook his head. "It's settled then." said Carl.

* * * * *

Everyone sat back down and quietly finished their meals. Mandy was the first to break the silence. "So, we are in agreement of *what* we want to do now, but how do we go about it?" she asked. "Well, the first thing we'll need to do is to get inside of that complex. I know Carl and Brian have seen it, but I think it would do more good if everyone could see it ... someone might get an idea from something that Carl or Brian may have overlooked." said Nick. "I agree." said Mandy. "Aren't we all forgetting something?" Amber interjected. "What?" asked Carl. "That somehow, they have the ability to track us." she said. "I had forgotten about that!" said Carl. "What is she talking about?" asked Nick. "You didn't know that? They can track us within what seems like a few feet!" exclaimed Mandy. "I couldn't lose them. How were you captured?" asked Keith. Nick's head tilted to the side as he began to think about Keith's question. "We got company!" yelled Brian as he stood up and pointed. There were three white vehicles approaching fast. "Let's go!" yelled Carl. Everyone scrambled for the white vehicle that they had arrived in. After everyone was securely inside, Carl took the driver's seat with Amber in the front, at his side. Carl headed down the road, away from the interstate. He pushed the vehicle as fast as he dared, so as to not lose control.

19

The Discovery

They had a very weak head-start. The pursuing vehicles were well within range if they had wanted to fire, but for some reason, they did not. Nick was standing in the cab of the vehicle just inside the doorway between the cab and the rear. "The ocean doesn't look so bad now, does it?" asked Carl jokingly. "I didn't know they could track us. Riding around in one of their vehicles isn't helping things much, either." said Nick. "I was just kidding. Young man, it is a far better thing you suggest we do than what I suggested. I just happen to think that as long as they have the ability to track us, we're not even going to make it to the complex." said Carl. "How do they do it? Human body heat or what?" shouted Nick rhetorically. Mandy walked from the rear of the vehicle into the cab. She put her hand on Nick's shoulder. He turned toward her, looked in her eyes briefly, then bowed his head. "I did all that talking about bravery, honor, and the right thing to do. Now, through my own ignorance, I've built up everyone's hopes, only to have them shatter and fall. I'm sorry." said Nick. "We're all in this together." said Mandy as she embraced the pained, young man. She was surprised when he quickly, but gently disengaged his embrace and pushed his way past her through the door into the rear of the vehicle. She looked at him in puzzlement. Nick had dropped down onto his hands and knees and reached under the bottom of Tracey's blue dress. He grabbed her ankle. Tracey tried to pull her leg away. Nick wouldn't let go. Tracey's silence held no longer. If she was ever in shock, she certainly wasn't now. At least, not the same kind. "What the heck do you think you're doing?" she yelled at Nick. Everyone was watching Nick's tug-of-war with Tracey's leg. "Nick, what *are* you doing?" asked Mandy. "Let me go!" yelled Tracey, finding her voice. She began to hit Nick with both of her hands. His hand came out from under her dress. He opened his hand, palm up. A gold watch sparkled from the bright, white light shining in the vehicle. "That belonged to someone very special me." said Tracey bluntly, as she calmed down and resumed her inattentiveness toward the group.

* * * * *

"So? I've got a watch too." said Mandy. "Just like this?" asked Nick as he handed it to her. "Yes, as a matter-of-fact, exactly like it." said Mandy with surprise. "So did I! That's what the alien called Strax had been holding when I first saw him! He was holding my watch. That's how they're tracking us! I bet every single one of us has one of these watches!" exclaimed Nick. "I've got one! My dad bought it for me on his trip to California. He got it really cheap." said Keith. "What about you, Preacher Briggs?" asked Nick. "I sure do. One of my flock gave it to me." he said. "Marty?" asked Nick. "That's ridiculous! They're not tracking us by our watches." said Marty. Nick walked to the back of the vehicle where Marty sat. He grabbed his arm and pulled up his suit sleeve. He pulled the watch off of Marty's wrist. "Hey! You can't do that!" yelled Marty as he stood up. Nick got in his face. "Can't I?" Nick asked. They stood face-to-face for a moment. "Boys!" exclaimed Mandy. Marty sat back down. Nick collected everyone's watches and then walked to the front of the cab. He held them all out in front of him to show them to Carl. "It's our watches, Carl! They're tracking us by our watches!" he exclaimed. Amber dug through her pocket and pulled out her father's watch. She looked at it with sadness, and then reluctantly handed it to Nick. "Good going, Nick!" said Carl. Brian walked up front to the cabin with Carl, Amber, and Nick. "Carl, I've got some bad news, buddy. They're not the only ones with a wrist piece." said Brian. He pulled the sleeve of the white radiation-type suit back and revealed his chrome-colored bracelet. "If I'm not mistaken, all of us that wear these nice, white suits have this required piece of jewelry." said Brian. "Oh, my! I've never even thought about that. I always figured that it was just to separate us from the other humans that did not have clearance in some of the restricted areas at the complex! Those blue monsters were tracking us all along!" exclaimed Carl.

20

It's Not What You Got

"We'll think of something." said Nick, addressing Carl's concern of their seemingly unremovable homing bracelets. "It's gonna have to be fast, they're catching up." said Carl. "Come on, let's put our heads together." said Nick as he walked back to the rear of the vehicle. Mandy followed him. Brian started to follow, but Carl halted him. "Amber, go on to the back and see if you can help them come up with any ideas. I need to talk to Brian." said Carl. "About what?" said Amber suspiciously. "The same thing. What to do about our bracelets. Now go on back, then let me know if you come up with anything." said Carl, sternly. Amber nodded and then got up from the passenger's chair in the cab, and went to the back of the vehicle where everyone was doing some brainstorming. She knew something was wrong. Brian sat down. Carl closed the door that separated the cab and the rear of the vehicle. "I think you know what I've got in mind." said Carl. "Pretty much. You and I are either getting ready to get captured or killed while the others escape, right?" asked Brian. "That's it exactly. Unless ... you would rather hold out for another way. But, we're running out of time." said Carl. "Of course, I wish there was another way, but I know that our separation from the rest of the group is going to be their only chance of survival. As long as you and I can be tracked, none of our plans will succeed." said Brian. Carl nodded in agreement. "So, what do you propose?" asked Brian. Carl gave Brian an overview of what he had in mind. When he finished, Brian said "I guess that's the best you could come up with on such short notice, huh?" Carl nodded. "We'll never know if it worked or not." said Brian. "Probably not, we'll both probably be dead." said Carl. "Let me know when you're ready." said Brian. He opened the door and walked back to the rear of the vehicle and listened to the other ideas. Brian knew that Carl's plan was the only one that would even come close to working. And even that plan was going to be shaky.

* * * * *

Nick entered the cab and sat down in the seat beside Carl. "Come up with anything?" Carl asked him. "Nothing tangible." said Nick quietly. "I have." said Carl. "Oh, yeah?" asked Nick. "Yeah, and I don't want to hear any protests when I tell you, either." said Carl. "Uhhh ... okay." said Nick, puzzled. Carl explained the plan. Nick was quiet for a moment before he responded. "Listen, there has to be a better way. Don't take all of that heroic talk I laying out completely to heart and go out of your head!" said Nick. "I told you no protests! This is the only way, but it won't work if you don't help! You started this take back our planet crap, and you darned well better finish it!" exclaimed Carl. They were both quiet. Carl spoke again. "Don't give Brian or I a second thought. You just see that the others are taken care of. That's priority one, okay?" said Carl as he held his free hand out to Nick. "Okay." said Nick as he clasped Carl's hand. "You and Brian make sure everyone's ready." said Carl. "Okay." said Nick. "Maybe Brian and I will somehow make it through this." said Carl. Nick nodded and then walked to the back of the vehicle.

* * * * *

Carl finally spotted the place he was looking for. A convenience store that still had backup power and gas pumps. He swung the vehicle in right next to the gas pumps. He and Brian ran into the store, carrying all of the watches from the group. Nick jumped out of the vehicle and grabbed a gas nozzle from one of the gas pumps. He flipped the pump on, and the numbers on the pump reset to zero. He fixed the nozzle where the handle would stay down, and gas began to pour out in a stream. He gently laid the nozzle on the ground, next to the pump. He climbed the ladder and was quickly back inside of the white vehicle. "Amber, take the driver's seat, but stay down, and wait until I say go." said Nick. He peeked out the door to see a pool of gas spreading around the pumps and parking lot of the convenience store. It was also pouring under their own vehicle. "Nobody light a match." said Nick with a chuckle.

* * * * *

A few moments later, two of the three pursuing vehicles quickly swung into the convenience store parking lot, right up next to the building. The third one drove around to the back of the building. There was a pictorial representation of the area on the computer screens inside of each of the vehicles. There were six flashing red dots and two flashing yellow dots in a cluster in the middle of the graphic that represented the convenience store on the computer screen. The two yellow dots were Carl and Brian. The six red dots were the watches that they carried. Strax had taken nick's watch from the debris at the Phoenix Mental Institution, so it was not among the group of watches. Nick carefully peeked out the open door of the white vehicle. He saw several white-suited figures posted outside of the store. Three of them looked as though they were preparing to go inside of the store. A few figures were milling around, as if anxious. One of them knelt down and looked at the gas puddle that was rapidly growing in size. Another suited figure inquisitively knelt down beside the first. As sudden comprehension and realization took hold of the two figures, they looked at each other and then stood up quickly. They sprinted toward the front of the store, where the other figures were standing and about to enter. Nick ran to the cab of the vehicle. "Take off!" he exclaimed to Amber. "But Carl and Brian aren't back yet!" Amber exclaimed. "Go, go, go!" Nick yelled at her as he grabbed ahold of the drive lever and pushed it forward himself. Everyone heard the squall of the tires and the screech of the tracks on the pavement. Nick was surprised that the tracks did not spark the gasoline. As the vehicle began to lean from the sudden speed and lack of steering, Amber grabbed the steering wheel and tried to straighten it out. She had not been fast enough. The vehicle had gone only a few hundred feet before it finally leaned over and fell on its side. Nick was thankful that the vehicle's doors were not blocked. He quickly pulled himself upward through the door of the overturned vehicle. When he was on top of it, he saw all of the suited figures running toward their own vehicles. He did not see Brian or Carl. He aimed the hand-held weapon that Carl had given him at the gas pump and fired.

* * * * *

There was a loud WHOOSH! The gasoline flames roared in the air. A moment later, there was an explosion. The gas pumps flew up into the air with a large orange, yellow, and red fireball coming from beneath them. The shifting, hot air wave hit Nick and propelled him off of the top of the overturned vehicle. The store blew apart like a dollhouse under the wheel of an asphalt compaction roller. Many smaller explosions erupted from the burning building. Because of their close proximity to the store and gas pumps, all three of the white, enemy vehicles, were each hit by the explosion force and flaming debris. All of them began to burn, and two of them exploded. The figures that had been running for their vehicles never had a chance. They were engulfed by the explosion. The overturned vehicle with the human passengers was pelted with debris. The sky around the store building was black with smoke.

The door to the back of the over-turned vehicle hissed open. Marty stumbled out as fast as he could. Mandy and Preacher Briggs were both helping Tracey, who was, again, in hysterics. Keith, using all of his strength, managed to carry Amber out of the vehicle. She was unconscious and had blood on her face. "Let's get further away from the fire." said Mandy. "Can you help her, Preacher?" asked Mandy. "Yes, I've got her." he said. Mandy released Tracey's other arm and ran to Nick, who was on the ground a few feet behind the vehicle. When she touched him, he opened his eyes. "Are you okay?" she asked. Nick was quiet for a moment. "Yeah, except for all the places I hurt." he said, rubbing the back of his head. Mandy kissed Nick on the cheek. Nick looked at her with astonishment and then said "Every little bit helps." As he smiled at her. Mandy helped him to his feet. Nick started toward the flaming ruination of the convenience store area, and Mandy gently grabbed his arm. "Brian and Carl . . ." he began. "Nick, no one survived that. It's too hot to even approach it right now." Mandy said, softly. Nick knew it to be true. He nodded slowly, and let Mandy lead him to meet the others, who were already walking down the road away from the inferno. Keith, who was already small for his age, was summoning all of his strength to carry Amber. She was also petite, but still a heavy load for him to carry. He wasn't about to let her down. Nick was leaning on Mandy, as he was walking with a limp. "I think I sprained my ankle." he said. Mandy looked at him and had a feeling inside of her that she had not felt in a very long time, but she didn't say anything. "Hey! Where are you guys going? Let's get off of the road. They may not be able to track us anymore, but let's not make it any easier for them to find us." Nick yelled to everyone up ahead of them. "Where do you want to go?" asked the preacher. Nick looked around. "That way for now, just for a few minutes." he said, pointing to a field next to the road. Everyone walked slowly into the field. Nick motioned for everyone to halt. Keith gently laid Amber onto the soft ground. Nick turned around and faced the direction of the burning gas station and vehicles, as they were still in view. "Let no one here forget this day. Carl Medwin and Brian Stanton gave their lives so that we all might live another day. So, we can fight for our freedom." said Nick with passion. "We will not let them down!" he shouted. As if in agreement, the last enemy vehicle exploded, causing everyone to flinch. As if one entity, the group slowly turned back around, and again faced the field. Keith carefully picked Amber back up, and the group began walking once more. As they walked, Nick explained to the group what Carl and Brian had planned to do back at the store.

There was a forest at the opposite edge of the field, and they went through it. After a short time of walking, they came out in a small rural area. A few quaint houses dotted the countryside along a dirt road that wound its way upward, through the woods. None had been spared from some kind of damage. "Let's not stop at the first house. Maybe the third or fourth." said Nick. They stopped at the third house. Although there was a large portion of one of the back walls missing, the house's structural integrity appeared to be sound.

21

A Little R & R

Keith found the nearest bedroom and gently placed Amber on the bed. Mandy helped Nick into a comfortable chair and then joined Keith. The preacher led Tracey to the couch and sat down beside her. Marty receded into a dark corner, sat down and drew his knees up against his chest. He leaned back against the wall and exhaled loudly. "There's plenty of room here on the couch." said Preacher Briggs to Marty. "I'm good." said Marty. "What's your problem?" Tracey snapped at Marty. Nick and the preacher were surprised to hear Tracey talking. "I don't have a problem! Do you?" asked Marty right back at her. "You're such a jerk!" exclaimed Tracey. "You don't have the right to call anyone anything! You're just a stuck-up snob!" exclaimed Marty. Marty and Tracey began spitting insults at each other. Preacher Briggs tried to intervene, but his calm demeanor yielded no result. "Quiet, dang it, quiet!" yelled Nick at the top of his lungs as he tried to stand up. "Oww!" he yelled as he quickly sat back down, having put too much pressure on his hurt foot. Mandy ran into the room. "Everyone! Please! Amber is waking up!" she exclaimed in a whisper. Everyone became silent.

* * * * *

Amber's face was clean and blood-free once again. Keith had assisted Mandy with cleaning the small gash on her forehead. She had a large, purple knot on her head where the gash was. When Amber opened her eyes, she found her companions all gathered around her. She remembered everything that had happened up until the vehicle had fallen on its side, and she had hit her head. "Carl?" she asked. "I'm very sorry." said Nick. Amber teared up. Keith held Amber's hand. Keith's own eyes teared up with sadness for the beautiful, young girl. Mandy placed her hand on Amber's head and stroked her hair. "How are you feeling?" Mandy asked. "I think I'm going to be okay." said Amber. "We were worried about you." said Nick. "What do *you* care?" asked Amber with anger. Although she had still been unconscious when Nick had explained to the group about Carl and Brian's plan, she knew in her heart that Nick had known Carl and Brian's intentions. "Listen, Amber ..." Nick began. When he made eye contact with her, it looked as if her gaze could burn a hole through him. He didn't even attempt to finish what he had planned to say, he just bowed his head, turned and then limped out of the room. "They did what they had to do. You shouldn't be so hard on Nick. He didn't like it any more than any of us did. It was the only way." said Preacher Briggs. The group filled her in on what Nick had told them about what Brian and Carl had planned. Amber understood it, but it didn't make her feel any better. "I think Amber needs some rest, guys. I'll be back to check on you." said Mandy. She left the room and everyone else followed. Everyone but Keith.

* * * * *

"Amber probably has a concussion. All we can do is wait, and hope it's nothing serious." said Mandy to Nick. Mandy had found Nick sitting outside in the grass, rubbing his hurt ankle. It was twilight, and there was a gentle breeze blowing. Nick remained quiet. Mandy sat down beside him. After they both sat quietly for a few minutes, Mandy finally said. "She knows it's not your fault, Nick. Give her some time." Nick didn't respond. Mandy put her arm on his shoulder. "Nick?" she said. Although Mandy's touch was wonderfully comforting to him, he was also preoccupied. "Shhh, wait just a minute. Listen." he said as he cocked his head to one side, listening. He had moved Mandy's arm from his shoulder and held her hand in both of his. Mandy remained quiet, listening as well. After a few moments, Nick said "Do you hear them?" Mandy pushed her long, black hair from off of her ears and also tilted her head sideways. "What am I listening for?" she asked. "I hear crickets!" exclaimed Nick. Mandy listened more intently, and realized she had heard them all along, only she had taken the common sound for granted. "I hear them too!" she exclaimed. "That's the first time I've heard another living thing besides us few people that actually belongs here on Earth." said Nick. "You know, you're right. Now that you mention it, I haven't seen or heard *anything* either. Why do you think we hear them now?" asked Mandy. "I don't know. But I'd like to take it as some kind of positive sign." said Nick. Mandy looked at Nick. They looked into each other's eyes as if searching. They leaned toward each other and kissed. It had been a long time since either of them had such feelings stir within. After the kiss, they looked into each other's eyes once again, and then instinctively hugged each other tightly. "Nick, I've been trying to be strong, but I'm so scared." said Mandy. "I'm scared too. I don't know why, but I've got a feeling deep inside of me that everything's going to be okay." he said. *As long as we're together.* Nick thought. He knew it had only been a very short time, but he wondered just exactly when he began to fall in love with this beautiful woman.

* * * * *

Keith had sat down in a chair next to Amber's bed. "I'll be okay."

said Amber. "I know you will." said Keith. After a short period of silence, Amber finally said "Thank you." Keith gave Amber a puzzled look. "For what?" he asked. "I wasn't completely unconscious the entire time. I know that you carried me all the way." she said. He looked down at his feet, turning red with embarrassment. "It was nothing." he said. "It was everything." she said. She reached out to Keith. He looked up questioningly. She stretched her arm all the way out, reaching with her open hand. He shyly took it. She squeezed his hand tight. He squeezed back. Keith felt as if he had aged from 15 to 25 over the past few days. Amber's gesture warmed his heart as it had never been warmed before, and he was having strange feelings that he was completely unfamiliar with.

* * * * *

They had spent the night in the house. The next day, Nick's foot was already feeling tremendously better. He and Preacher Briggs had scouted out the neighboring houses to see what they could find along the lines of breakfast for everyone. They couldn't get any re-frigerated or frozen foods, because they feared that they may have begun spoiling. There was, however, plenty of non-perishable foods throughout most of the homes. There were plenty of canned goods, some of which had some meats of different varieties in them. None of them were able to eat like a king, but they knew that there would most likely be plenty of canned goods and non-perishables to be found for some years to come. Many items may would eventually be beyond the best-by date, but would still be edible. *That is, if we're still around.* Nick thought. Nick and the preacher had each come back with a large sack full of food. They emptied the contents onto the kitchen table.

* * * * *

Keith waited on Amber hand and foot. He was glad to do it. She insisted that she felt as if she could get up and around, but Mandy only let her get up to go to the bathroom. Water for the toilet had to be carried from a creek that flowed a few hundred yards away from the house. They drank bottled water and soft drinks that they had put in the creek to cool.

A week passed and Amber was significantly better. With her assurance that she was okay to travel, Nick decided that it was a good time for them to begin moving once again. They followed the rural roadway of the neighborhood they were in. They collected plenty of food and other supplies from the houses along the way. For the most part, they were all working together as a team.

The ordeal of the past few weeks had brought the companions closer together. Interpersonal relationships inside of the group had begun to strengthen. Keith and Amber were holding hands. Nick and Mandy had their arms around each other's shoulders. Preacher Briggs talked away while Tracey smiled and nodded in all the right places. Each person carried a bag of supplies with them. Marty usually dragged behind the group and rarely spoke to anyone.

* * * * *

The group came to an intersection. They had not yet found a vehicle they could travel in. The dirt road they were traveling on continued on the other side of a much larger, four-lane highway. "I think we should cross the highway and stay fifty feet or so into the woods, as we follow the road. We need to get more distance between us and that gas station before we can start to feel a little safer about traveling on a main road again. They're really going to be looking for us now." said Nick. They crossed the highway and went into the woods, just deep enough where they could see back out to the road. "Maybe they'll think we died with everyone else in the fire." said Keith. "It's possible, but they probably have one heck of a forensics team." said Mandy. "Where are we going, anyway?" asked Tracey. "Michigan." said Nick. "Why there?" she asked. "That's where one of their bases are." said Amber. "What are we going to do when we get there?" Tracey asked. "We're all going to die, that's what we're going to do!" exclaimed Marty from behind the group. Nick put his bag of supplies down on the ground and left Mandy's side. "What're you doing, Nick?" asked Mandy. "I'm sick and tired of hearing him!" snapped Nick. "Nick ..." Mandy began.

Marty began to back away from Nick, as he approached, as he could see the fury in his eyes. "You've got no right . . ." said Marty as he stumbled backward, onto the ground, dropping his bag of supplies. "The heck I don't! I've had about enough of you! We're all scared enough as it is without your constant comments about our impending doom! If you don't want to go, then you don't have to. But, if you're going to stay with this group, you're going to stop dragging everyone down!" said Nick as he turned back around and looked back at the group. They had all stopped and were watching Nick confront Marty. Nick continued. "I'll go by myself if I have to. I don't want to, but I will. But, if anyone wants to call it off, then say so now. I need to know who I can depend on." said Nick as he looked at each of their faces. "Nick, none of us deserve being talked to like that. We *all* said we were with you." said Mandy sourly. "No, everyone hasn't said it. But I am now. I'm with you, Nick." said Tracey, to everyone's surprise. Nick nodded with strange pride. "I know most of you are willing to do this and have said so. I apologize for any negative implications, but we actually *all* need to know that we can depend on each other." said Nick. He turned around and faced Marty again. "This is the last time I want to talk to you about this. You make up your mind ... *now!*" snapped Nick. "Okay, okay. I just don't think ..." began Marty. "The fact that you don't think we can do it doesn't matter! Just stop saying it and try to have a positive attitude!" Nick yelled. "Okay, I won't say anything else to anyone." said Marty. Nick squatted down in front of Marty. "No, Marty. That's not what I want you to do, either. I just want you to stop being so pessimistic. If you can't stop being pessimistic, at least stop making everyone else feel that way. I happen to think we're going to make a difference. I want everyone to feel that way, including you, Marty!" said Nick as he stood up. Marty was silent for a few moments. "I'm scared, Nick." said Marty as he began to sob. "We all are, Marty. And there's nothing wrong with that." said Nick. Marty stared down at his feet. Tracey went to him, squatted down, and put an arm around his neck. "Everything's all gone, isn't it?" Marty sobbed. "I know how you feel. You all saw that I had trouble coming to terms with it, too. I just handled it differently than you did." said Tracey. She held him until he seemed to have gathered his composure. "Thank you." he said. "I've come to realize that we do all have to stick together. We may be all that each other's got." she said. After Marty composed himself, everyone picked up their bags and continued onwards, through the woods, alongside the road.

22

New Set of Wheels

Nick stopped walking and his face had lit up. "What is it?" asked Mandy. They had just begun descending a grassy field when Nick's sharp eyes caught a glimpse of something. "Look!" he exclaimed, pointing across the field through a clearing in some trees. The group spotted what appeared to be a school building, but they were unsure exactly why it had excited Nick. Before they had the chance to allow him to elaborate, he shouted "Come on!" and he broke into a run toward the school, as he grabbed Mandy's hand and dragged her along with him. Keith and Amber ran together, also holding hands. Preacher Briggs, Tracey and Marty all looked at each other. Tracey shook her head. "Yeah, I think I'll walk, too." said Marty. "If whatever it is survived these catastrophic events, I'm sure it can survive a few more minutes." said John Briggs. The three of them walked down the grassy field toward the school in the clearing.

* * * * *

"It's great! Just what we need!" exclaimed Nick as he ran to the back of one of the big, orange school buses, looking in the seats. He jumped into the very back seat and ducked out of sight. Mandy was at the front of the bus. She waited for Nick to reappear. Keith and Amber climbed the steps and stood behind Mandy. "Where's Nick?" asked Keith. "He's in the back of the bus, playing." said Mandy. "So, Nick, did you ride a bus to school?" asked Amber. There was no response. Mandy looked at Keith and Amber with a half-worried, half-irritated look on her face. "Nick?" she asked. No response. "Nick!" exclaimed Keith. Still, no response. "Nick, this isn't funny." said Mandy as she squatted down to look under the seats toward the back of the bus. She didn't see his feet. "Nick!" she exclaimed as she hurried to the back of the bus with Amber and Keith following behind her. As she neared the rear of the bus, Nick jumped up from out of the seat and began playfully pelting them with small wads of paper he had retrieved from the floor. Mandy let out a small scream. Nick stopped throwing the paper. The smile disappeared from his face. "Real funny, Nick." said Mandy as she sat down into a seat with exasperation. "I'm sorry, I was only playing." said Nick as he approached the seat Mandy was sitting in. He sat down and held up his index finger to Keith and Amber indicating that he wanted a moment alone with Mandy. "Come on, Keith." said Amber as she clasped his hand and led him from the bus. Nick put his arms around Mandy and held her. She looked away from him. "Mandy, please don't be upset. I'm sorry." said Nick pleadingly. "Some ... sometimes I ... I wonder what can be going thr ... through your head." said Mandy as she began to cry. "So did all the doctors." said Nick flatly. "What do you mean?" asked Mandy with a change in tone. "Nothing." said Nick. "Don't say that!" exclaimed Mandy. Nick was silent for a few moments. "I was a mental patient, Mandy." said Nick. "Why didn't you tell me?" asked Mandy. Nick was silent again. "For one thing, I was scared you might not like me anymore. Before all of this happened, I just can't see a beautiful woman like you even giving me the time of day, especially after knowing that. For another, I didn't want you to treat me any differently. If you're mad at me be mad. If you're happy, then show it. But I don't ever want you walking on eggshells worrying about my state of mind." said Nick. "I wouldn't *have* thought any differently of you, and I still don't. A lot of people need help like that." said Mandy. He looked into her eyes. "Do you really mean that?" asked Nick. "Of course, I do." said Mandy. See hugged him tightly and he returned the squeeze. "I am sorry, though. I guess I should have known better than acting like that with everything that's happened. Another time, maybe it would have been funny, but now really isn't the best time, huh? What a turn of events. I've actually got six people who are looking to me, a mental patient, for guidance. I guess I should try and straighten up my act a little." he said softly. "You seem pretty normal to me ... actually, you seem very intelligent." said Mandy. "Why thank you. Intelligence and psychological problems don't really have anything to do with each other, though, you know." said Nick. Mandy nodded. "I promise I won't keep anything else from you." said Nick. Mandy was quiet. "What's wrong?" asked Nick. "I need to tell you something too." said Mandy as she pulled away from him. "What's wrong?" Nick asked with concern from her sudden distantness and change of demeanor. Mandy paused before she began to speak. She looked away from him and bowed her head. "Nick, I was a prostitute." she said. Nick was quiet for a moment. Before he could speak, Mandy interjected "I took precautions, and it's probably not exactly the situation that you may think. It's not like I walked the streets or anything." said Mandy. "Mandy ..." Nick tried to speak when she cut him off. "I know. It was dumb. I'll understand if you don't want to touch me again." said Mandy, her head still bowed, looking away from him. Nick grabbed her and forced her to look at him. "Don't ever say that. We've all made mistakes. I don't think any less of you, Mandy. In fact, I ... I love you." said Nick. He kissed her. Nick felt her reciprocation in the kiss, and his spirit was electrified. Mandy also felt a tingle within her, along with a feeling of lightness from the release of the burdensome secret she had been carrying. After their kiss, through her tears of joy, she embraced him and whispered in his ear "And I love you."

* * * * *

"Where's Nick and Mandy?" asked Tracey as she, Marty, and Preacher Briggs met Keith and Amber in front of the bus. "Right here." said Nick as he followed Mandy down the bus steps. "What were you guys doing in there?" asked Tracey with a smile. She stopped smiling when they approached. Everyone saw the tears in both of their eyes. "I'm sorry, I was just kidding. Are you two okay?" Tracey said. "Couldn't be better." said Nick, smiling. "We've all been through a lot. Nick and I thought that we would get some of it out in the open. I know I feel better." said Mandy as she wiped at her tears with the back of her hand. "I do too." said Nick. Everyone was quiet. Marty broke the silence. "So, what kind of shape is this bus in?" he asked. "The inside looks fine. I totally forgot to check the engine." said Nick as he went back into the bus. The key was in the ignition. He sat down and turned the key. The bus fired up without a hitch. The group cheered. "Hey, Nick, we're going to go have a look around in the school." said Keith. "Okay. See if you can find a broom and some cleaning supplies." Nick responded. "We will." said Amber. Keith and Amber went into the school building. Nick began picking up trash on the bus. Mandy helped him. Preacher Briggs stepped into the bus. "What can we do to help out?" he asked. Nick looked at him for a moment. "We're going to need some gas." said Nick. "Okay. Anything else?" asked the Preacher. "That's all I can think of for now, thanks." said Nick. John Briggs nodded and then stepped off of the bus. The preacher told Marty and Tracey to split up and see what they could find.

23

Kaletta

A flying vehicle landed in front of the smoking, charred ruins of the convenience store. It was able to travel as a VTOL vehicle does. Several aliens and humans got out of the vehicle and began to look around. The aliens were donned with some kind of military attire. All of the humans were wearing the familiar white suits. They carefully walked around the crater that the gasoline tanks had made when they had exploded. A human stepped into the middle of the smoking ruins of the convenience store. He took out a sample jar and started to scoop some of the ash into it. An alien approached him and instructed him to stop. The alien was female. She had long, flowing silver hair. Not like a human's hair, but hers had the appearance as if it was a soft, malleable alloy. Her build was much like that of a human female. Although her facial features were similar to her male counterpart, her pointed conical teeth were much smaller, but unlike the male's stained teeth, hers were bright white and unblemished. She was very beautiful. She wore a small, decorative cape, and the many alien insignias on her uniform seemed to imply that she was the highest rank amongst the group. "Don't we need to take samples of the remains?" asked the human. The alien shook her head. "We don't have any way of tracking them, now. All of the transmitters are here. It no longer matters if all of the humans are dead or not. The collection was important, but it wasn't a necessity. Now, it is no longer a high priority." said the alien in a melodic voice, much more pleasant than the male's guttural sound. The human nodded and tossed the jar into the ruins of the convenience store.

"I've got something!" shouted one of the aliens in English. Several of the aliens and humans met the shouting alien at the over-turned vehicle. They all began talking amongst themselves. When the female alien approached, everyone quietened down. "I've found tracks and small traces of human blood leading up the side of the road." said the first alien to Kaletta. She nodded. "Very good, it is noted." she said as she turned away. "Kaletta ... shall I make preparations for pursuit?" asked the alien. "No. The evidence you have found is a good find, but it is insufficient to merit pursuance. The spare humans are no longer a major concern." said Kaletta without turning back around. "But, Kaletta, we were instructed..." the alien began. Kaletta turned back around sharply. "I am in charge here! Are you questioning my orders?" Kaletta snapped sharply. "No, Kaletta." said the alien as he quickly bowed his head forward in apology. "Prepare to disembark. There is nothing to do here." she said. The aliens and humans boarded the flying vehicle. Kaletta looked around one last time before she boarded the aircraft. The aircraft hovered into the sky and then sped away.

24

On the Road Again

Tracey had found cans of gasoline that went to the school's lawn mowers. Preacher Briggs had siphoned gasoline from some older model cars parked around the school. Marty hadn't found anything. Amber and Keith had found some cleaning supplies and had cleaned the interior of the school bus. Nick, Mandy, and Marty loaded some supplies and the extra cans of gasoline into the rear of the bus. Marty was beginning to become a part of the team. "I hope the gasoline fumes don't choke us to death." said Mandy. "They're sealed pretty good, but we can keep some of these back windows open to help with ventilation." said Marty. "Good thinking." said Nick.

* * * * *

"Are you going to be our DD?" Nick asked Amber. "DD?" she asked. "Designated Driver." said Marty. "Well ..." said Amber, glancing at Keith. Preacher Briggs sensed Amber's reluctance to leave Keith's side. "I don't mind driving the bus, Nick." said the preacher. "Okay, Preacher." said Nick. Everyone randomly piled into the seats around the bus. Amber and Keith sat together. Mandy and Nick sat together. Marty and Tracey sat together. Although it may have been through untraditional methods, and possibly primarily the circumstances they were in, the group's bond seemed to be growing stronger, along with the interpersonal relationships inside of it. They began finding the silver linings inside of each other. John Briggs started the bus. John was thankful that the bus had an automatic transmission. The preacher steered the bus from the school grounds.

* * * * *

There was no light to be seen anywhere, except for their own head lamps. The preacher had driven them safely to the interstate, dodging all of the dangerous wreckage and some newly formed small fissures in the earth. They were heading north. Destination: Michigan. Several times, the preacher was forced to switch sides of the highway in order to avoid colossal automobile wrecks on the interstate. Fortunately, there was always a way to get around on the wide stretch of interstate right-of-way. The steady hum of the bus engine was like music to the tired ears of the group. Everyone fell asleep, trusting the preacher to take them on a safe voyage.

* * * * *

It was four in the morning when the flying machine came down, almost on top of the bus. It swooped down in front of the bus, and slowed to match the large vehicle's sluggish speed. Not really knowing what else to do, Preacher Briggs stomped down on the brake. The tires squalled and the bus began to slide sideways. The preacher amazingly kept it from turning over. The flying vehicle landed no sooner than the bus had come to a complete stop, blocking the path forward. Everyone that was asleep on the bus was now wide awake and looking to Nick. He could see fear in their faces and an expectation of a directive. He shrugged his shoulders as he yelled "I guess we run for it!" Everyone scrambled toward the front of the bus, as the rear emergency exit was blocked by supplies. They met Preacher John Briggs standing at the end of the aisle. The glow of the instrumental panel revealed the cold eyes of the Preacher. The sudden appearance of the flying vehicle had triggered a change. He was no longer the kindly preacher, but the other personality. A cruel, deranged madman.

For the first time in his life, Marty was thinking of someone other than himself. Marty was still, as usual, at the front of the group. This time, however, he had pulled Tracey in front of him, in an effort to get her safely off of the bus as quickly as possible. "Open the door!" exclaimed Marty as he and Tracey approached. The preacher back-handed Tracey. She fell back, into Marty's arms. He had hit her so hard, her nose started to bleed. "Tracey!" exclaimed Marty as he examined her face. The others were in shock at the preacher's behavior. "I'm okay ... " she said nasally as she held her nose. Marty quickly pulled her back away from the preacher as the group moved back with him. She gained her own footing, and Marty saw that she was in control of herself. He headed back up the aisle, toward the preacher. "You dirty freak!" he exclaimed. "Welcome to the Promised Land." said the preacher as he grabbed Marty by the throat and swung his head against one of the metal sides of the bus, below the windows. He repeatedly smashed Marty's head against the metal. Marty struggled, but was no match for the bigger, stronger preacher. The entire group had moved forward to try to help Marty, but the small aisle down the center of the bus made it difficult to get to him in time. Marty's body went limp after a few seconds of the preacher's repeated hammering. The Preacher released Marty and his body slumped to the floor. Tracey screamed. "Oh my God." said Nick in a whisper as he thought twice about trying to over-power the big man. Nick held his arms outward and slowly began to backup and motioned for everyone else to do the same. "Oh, you'll see *Him* very soon." said John Briggs, having heard Nick's comment.

"Preacher, snap out of it!" yelled Keith. "Sinners! You're all a bunch of sorry sinners! He died for you, though. You'll all go to Heaven if you believe that. Do you believe?" said the Preacher rhetorically. The Preacher began to walk toward the group as they continued backing away, hitting the dead end of the supplies against the back of the bus. "He died for you ... now it's time for you to die for him!" he exclaimed. "John ... think about what you're doing." said Nick as he tried to reason with him. "Do yoooou wuh ..." the preacher drawled out. ". . . Belieeeve uh ..." he said with conviction. "... In Jeeeeesus?" John finished his broken sentence, having sounded like a familiar TV evangelist. Everyone frantically looked around for a weapon. Nothing useful or practical could be found.

25

Into the Fire?

They were all pressed against the back of the bus as the preacher approached. "We're probably going to have to kill him to stop him." said Nick. "Who's to say that we *can* kill him? He broke that alien's neck like it was a piece of uncooked spaghetti!" Mandy exclaimed. "And he handled poor Marty like a rag doll!" Amber exclaimed She glanced behind her and then began quickly snatching up supplies and propelling them toward the preacher. "The emergency door!" she exclaimed. Everyone else quickly followed suit and began throwing supplies at John. His was forced to slow his pace, as he had to deflect items that were being hurled at him as fast as the group could do so. The exit door was soon revealed and cleared to access. Amber grabbed the handle and pulled it. The door opened easily. They all quickly filed out the back door opening, scrambling over some of their supplies.

* * * * *

When they were all out, they began to run in the opposite direction of where they knew the alien aircraft to be. They barely got a few feet when they halted. There were six aliens that had already maneuvered around to the other side of the bus, blocking their retreat. Nick bowed his head and shook it slowly. "Out of the frying pan ..." he said. "... into the fire." Mandy completed his sentence.

The preacher burst out of the back of the bus and circled around in pursuit of the group. "Shall we gather at the river ..." he sang out loud as he headed toward Amber, the closest person to him. Keith quickly stepped in front of her and prepared himself for the large man's impact. A beam of light came from several hundred feet from the other side of the bus. It struck the preacher and he fell flat, only a few feet in front of Keith and Amber. None of the aliens moved. None of the humans moved. There was a heavy silence in the air, as the humans looked in the direction from which the beam had come from. They heard footfalls approaching from where the shot had been fired. The shoes clicked and clacked on the asphalt pavement. Her silver hair sparkled when she stepped by the beams of the bus headlamps. When she approached, the humans were in awe at how beautiful this alien was. "I am Kaletta. I am here to help you." she said in her unique, melodic voice.

* * * * *

They were all dumbfounded. No one said a word. Kaletta approached the group of humans. She looked at Tracey. "Why are you crying? I'm not going to hurt you." Kaletta said to Tracey. Kaletta walked over to Mandy. "You do not appear to be as scared as the other females. Why?" she asked. Mandy did not respond. Kaletta looked at Nick. "You ... there's something different about you." she said as she approached him. "I'm not sure how to interpret the look on your face." Kaletta added. Nick was quiet for a moment. "I've got to pee." he said with a deliberate Southern drawl. Everyone was quiet at first. Mandy put her hand on her mouth and began trying to stifle the laughter that she was spitting through her lips.

Keith began to snicker. Nick let go of his straight face and threw his head back and began to roar with laughter. Amber started to laugh. Tracey, even upset, began to giggle at the blatant, silly remark Nick made in such a serious situation. They all began to laugh very hard. Mandy was holding her stomach. Keith was laughing so hard. he could no longer stand. He dropped to the ground. Amber was about to pee her pants for real. They had been through so much together, it was as if they were all having a mental break down at the same time. To their surprise, Kaletta even began to laugh with them. After several minutes, the laughter died down. There were tears in everyone's eyes. Kaletta extended her hand down to Keith, who still on the ground. He hesitated, and then took it. She was very strong, and had no trouble pulling him right up. "Thank you." said Keith. "You're welcome." she said as she backed away to face the whole group of humans. "I am here to take you all to a safe place." said Kaletta. "Why? And how do we know this is not some kind of trick?" asked Mandy. "We could have killed or captured you at any time, I assure you." said Kaletta. "Well, that's not very convincing." said Nick. "And why not?" asked Kaletta. "I'm sure that's what the rest of your people thought. You know, the ones that *we* have relieved of *their* lives!" exclaimed Nick with anger. Kaletta was silent for several moments. "I can't possibly know the pain and hatred that you have in you now. I can understand it, though. My people have committed a terrible crime. Almost complete extinction of your race ..." began Kaletta. "So its true? We are the last humans alive?" asked Keith. "No, there are more, but only a fraction as compared to your planet's original population. There are some that are unwilling captives. They won't last long under the tests and experiments. Most, however, are now servants that gladly comply to assure the safety of themselves and their families." said Kaletta. "They are traitors!" exclaimed Nick. "I would not judge your fellow species to harshly in that respect. In this way, our species are very much alike. We want to protect our families and will do anything to do so. As far as being a traitor goes, I am being one to my people in order to help you." Kaletta said. "It's not the same." said Nick. "Does it matter?" she asked. Nick was silent. Keith began to sniffle and fight against his tears from the news Kaletta had brought them. Amber held him. Tracey began to cry. Nick and Mandy both went to her and tried to comfort her. Kaletta ordered her men back into the aircraft. Deep down, from everything they had witnessed, and the fact that the only humans they had seen were themselves, they already knew the truth about their population. Kaletta turned and walked onto the bus. The group waited for her, feeling only apathy. When she returned, she gave the humans a few minutes to calm down before she continued. "From what I witnessed, I assume that the man I disabled is responsible for the death of the man on this multi-passenger vehicle." said Kaletta. "He's dead?" Tracey asked, beginning to sob again. "I'm afraid so." said Kaletta. "Yes, the man you shot is responsible." said Mandy. "Why did he do it?" asked Kaletta. "We don't really know. We think there is something wrong with his mind." said Nick. "A mental illness?" Kaletta asked. Although they shouldn't be based upon their obvious technological advancements, they were still surprised at her vast knowledge on a variety of subjects. Nick noticed Mandy looking at him. She gripped his hand. "Do you wish to kill him?" Kaletta asked. "No!" Nick exclaimed. "We just need to make sure he doesn't hurt anyone else." said Nick. "We will bind him, then. We need to get moving as soon as possible." said Kaletta. Keith helped Nick lift the preacher from the ground and began to head toward the alien aircraft. "Exactly how do you plan to help us?" Amber asked Kaletta. "I'm going to find you a safe and undisclosed area in which to live during my people's colonization. Once they have completed colonization, then I will come for you and find another pleasant, safe, and undisclosed area that you might live out the remainder of your lives as comfortably as possible." she said. Nick stopped dead in his tracks and motioned for Keith to lay the preacher back down on the ground, as he did so himself. He walked back to where Kaletta was standing. "Whoa, there. That's not exactly what we want. We're not zoo animals, to be kept somewhere!" exclaimed Nick. "What exactly do you mean?" asked Kaletta. "We want to be free. We're taking it back." said Nick. "Taking what back?" asked Kaletta. "Our planet." said Nick.

* * * * *

Kaletta began laughing. She had not intended to insult Nick, but the thought of his implication seemed very implausible. She ceased when she saw that Nick was not returning her jocularity. "You are sincere?" she asked. "Dang straight." said Nick. "There are not many of my people left, that is why we are here and have committed this atrocious act. But you're still only a few people against many. What can you possibly expect to accomplish?" asked Kaletta. "That's not the point. We'll die trying, if that's what it takes. That's what truly makes us human." said Nick. "No. It's what makes you foolish." said Kaletta. "Well, you may as well be on your way, then. I guess I need to thank you for not killing us, but if you're not going to help us, just leave us be." said Mandy. Nick nodded to Mandy in agreement, proud of the way she commented. Kaletta was silent. After a moment, she finally said "Very well." She turned away and walked back toward her aircraft. Nick walked over to Keith, who was still standing by the unconscious preacher. They began carrying him back toward the school bus. Kaletta turned around. "Wait. I can get you inside of the complex that I am assigned to without detection, but that's as far as I can go." she said. Nick smiled. He and Keith headed back toward the aircraft, carrying the preacher along with them. Tracey, Mandy, and Amber joined them. When they got to the entrance, Nick asked Mandy to help Keith get the preacher inside. He then asked Kaletta for her weapon. "Why do you want my weapon?" she asked. "I've got some last rites to take care of." said

Nick. Kaletta looked at him questioningly and suspiciously, but as a symbol of trust relinquished her weapon. Nick walked back to the bus and went in. He set the weapon on its most powerful setting, then fired it at Marty's body. It crackled, popped, and then disappeared in a flash of sparks. "You were really turning thins around, buddy. I wish you could have made it through this with us." he said as he switched the bus engine off and turned it's lights out. He headed back to the aircraft.

26

Free Ride

The Preacher had been securely bound, and was still unconscious. The group of humans marveled at the technology inside of the alien aircraft. It was unlike anything any of them had ever seen. Its design was very similar to the interior of a human designed aircraft, only everything was cleaner, less jumbled, and digital. There were buttons, dials, and gauges, just as on an ordinary plane, only they were all recessed, flat on their appropriate control panels. There were no windows. The viewport was like a giant curved, computer monitor displaying a live image from what they supposed was an alien camera somewhere on the outside of the craft. There were several other video panels that showed many different views from the craft. The seats were plain in design, but sat very comfortably. There were no ornamental symbols, brand names, or other markings, only necessities. Amber was carefully watching the pilot navigate the aircraft. She quickly understood how to pilot the ship. "A child could do it." Amber said aloud. "What?" asked Keith. "A child could fly this ship." Amber said. "Hear that, Nick? Amber already knows how to fly this thing." said Keith. Nick looked at Amber and stared at her. Nick's mind began to wander and his eyes glazed over. *You're only a few people against many. What can you possibly expect to accomplish?* Kaletta had said. He was beginning to ask himself that same question, as he looked around at the sophisticated equipment. Is he needlessly sacrificing all of their lives? Maybe zoo life was not so bad. *Remember, that's not the point.* Nick told himself. "Nick? You okay?" Amber asked. Nick snapped out of his daze. "Uh, yeah. You know how to fly it already, huh?" he asked her. "Yep, Its like taking candy from a baby." she said. "Good. We may be visiting a candy store." said Nick with a wink. Amber smiled.

* * * * *

They had been in flight for only a few minutes, and had traversed all the way across the United States when Kaletta announced that they were almost at the complex. They were all amazed at the remarkable speed of the sophisticated craft. "Why weren't these air vehicles used to go after us?" Nick asked Kaletta. "Your collection was a low priority. Even so, a thorough field examination could not be performed touching down from place to place in this military craft. They also wanted to do some exploration of your world." she responded.

* * * * *

The humans watched in awe as the aircraft approached Lake Superior, a few miles off of Keweenaw Point. The water began to bubble and ripple as a platform rose up out of the deep water. The aircraft hovered above. As the remaining water was channeled aside, the center of the platform opened up. Once the aircraft had hovered down inside, the platform closed once again. It then began to descend back down into the water. "Man!" exclaimed Keith in a whisper. Everyone in the group was wide-eyed with wonder.

27

The Complex

Once the vehicle was down inside of a large bay, the pilot gently hovered it over to a spot next to several other aircraft. The aircraft was completely void of any kind of engine noises. After the vehicle settled gently to the floor, Nick asked to speak with Kaletta in private. She led him back to a small room, which looked like a strategic planning area. "What about your six men? How are you going to keep them from turning us in?" asked Nick. "Those men are completely loyal to *me*. We have all been through a lot together. You may not believe it, Nick, but not all of my people agreed with how command approached your world. I have others who are loyal to me in the complex. A lot of them also did not agree with command's final decision." said Kaletta, with a remorseful look on her face. Nick slowly nodded with comprehension. He had many ideas and feasible scenarios of things that could have been done differently, that he briefly thought about saying. It was a now a moot point. *No sense bringing things up, especially when she's willing to help us.* Nick thought. "You and your companions stay put for now. I'll be back a little later, when the patrol shift changes, and some of my people are on duty." said Kaletta. "Okay. Why do you have so many followers? Is it an organization of some kind?" asked Nick. "I'm part of what you would call an *underground* group that did not want to take over your world in this way. But your planet was our last chance of survival. Our scientist were working on a project to safely transport all of your people into controlled facilities ..." Kaletta said as Nick interrupted her. "Prisons." he said. "Yes, prisons. Command decided not to approach any of your world's governments, as that would spoil the element of surprise, if we would not be helped. Our situation was very desparate. The project to transport your people failed. Even though we are well ahead of your race in technology, the matter transporter technologies are still in their infancy. Your people were not being dematerialized properly, which also meant that they were not rematerializing properly. Oblivious of the fact that they were basically committing populicide, they continued anyway. This was acceptable to some of my people." said Kaletta, looking down. "What about the watches?" asked Nick. "Those were placed by operatives in order to make sure some humans were not transported. Fortunately for you and your companions, they worked. There was going to be a study, to find out if there were any detrimental effects to living organisms around the dematerialization streams." said Kaletta. "I haven't seen any animals." said Nick. "Yes, that was another flaw in the project. The scan was originally supposed to seek out human form, dematerialize them and safely rematerialize them to selected coordinates. Instead, it ended up dematerializing most life, and not bringing it back. We don't know what happened to the animals. That is still a mystery." said Kaletta. Nick bowed his head. "I know this doesn't mean much to you, Nick, but I am sorry for what my people have done and there are others like me that feel the same way." said Kaletta. Nick did not respond. He was not quite sure if he was ready to offer the absolution that Kaletta may have desired. They left the planning room and joined the others. "I'll be back as soon as I can." said Kaletta. She and the other aliens left the aircraft.

* * * * *

The preacher awakened during Kaletta's absence. "Why am I tied up?" he asked. Mandy sat down beside him. "You don't remember a thing, do you?" she asked. "Yes, I remember everything. We were in a wreck ... and I guess I got knocked unconscious." he said. "We didn't actually wreck. You weren't knocked unconscious." said Mandy. "What are you talking about? Did I pass out?" he asked. "Preacher Briggs, this is a hard thing to have to tell someone ..." Mandy began. "What? What is it?" he quickly asked when he saw the dread in her eyes. "You've got a split personality or something. You killed Marty." she said. "No. That's impossible." the preacher said as he shook his head. "It's true. If things didn't work out like they did, you may have killed us all." said Keith. Preacher Briggs was quiet. "I'm sorry. I think we all kind of suspected something since the incident at the bridge. You turned and pointed your weapon at us, after killing Strax. We all thought you were going to shoot us. You had a strange, vacant look on your face. Just like tonight ..." said Mandy. "Oh, no. I killed him? Oh, no ... no, no, no ..." the preacher said as he lowered his head down and rested his chin on his chest and began to quietly sob. Mandy put her hand on his shoulder. "Forgive me Father, I knew not what I did." he whispered.

* * * * *

Kaletta returned within three hours. She was carrying white radiation-type suits for everyone. "These will allow you to get around to many places inside of the complex. There are certain areas that are restricted to humans, and I advise you against even trying to get in them. Of course, I have a feeling you're not going to be *asking* anyone to let you into those areas." said Kaletta as she passed out the suits.

"What about Preacher Briggs?" Mandy asked. Nick squinted his eyes and frowned with thought. "Somebody's going to have to stay with him. We can't just leave him here, tied up, alone." said Amber. "Did you just volunteer?" Mandy asked. Amber looked at Keith. He shrugged his shoulders. "I guess I did." said Amber. "Good." said Mandy. "Kaletta, how long will your men be patrolling this area during their shift?" Nick asked her. "For the next eight hours." she said. Everyone stood silently for several moments. "Thank you for all of your help, Kaletta." Mandy said, offering her hand. Kaletta shook hands all around with the humans. She removed two weapons from her belt and placed them in Nick's hands. "Good luck. Regardless of what happens, I am probably going to be in a lot of trouble." she said as she smiled. Tracey, who usually tried to avoid involving herself in the group's conversations, surprised everyone. "Why don't you join us?" she exclaimed. Kaletta thought for a moment. "I can't do it. Even though I'm helping you, I just couldn't actively go against my people." she finally said. "Well, you can at least be ready to come with us when we leave." said Tracey. "Leave here? The only way you can leave here is by leaving now. I will try to have someone here to open the upper platform door, but once you're discovered, it won't be long at all until you are captured or killed." said Kaletta. "We'll see about that." said Keith boldly. Nick nodded with pride. That's just the attitude we need to pull this thing off. Nick thought. "One more thing ... you can find out if you're talking to one of my loyalists by saying the word *mohtaka*. If it's one of my people, they will respond by responding with the word *tohmondra*. If it's my people, tell them what you need. If they can give it to you, they will." said Kaletta. "What if it's not one of your people? How will they respond to that word?" Nick asked. "It will just be gibberish to them. They may even think it's a strange human word!" she said. She again wished them luck and then left the bay.

* * * * *

Everyone got suited up. Keith gave Amber a hug. Mandy raised Preacher Briggs' head from where his chin rested on his chest and forced him to look at her. "We're leaving now, Preacher. I'm sorry we've got to keep you tied up." said Mandy. John avoided looking into her eyes. "I understand." he said. "Listen, I can't imagine how you feel right now, but know that none of us hate you. You need some kind of help, and we're not able to give it to you right now." said Mandy. The preacher did not respond. "He does forgive you, Preacher. You more than anyone should know that." said Mandy as she squeezed his shoulder. "Hang tight, Ace." said Nick to Amber. "I will. You guys be careful." she said. Nick, Mandy, Keith, and Tracey all left the ship. Nick hid one of the weapons Kaletta had given him under his suit. He handed the other to Mandy. She hid her weapon as well. The four humans walked out of the bay into another area of the complex.

* * * * *

They were in awe at the great span of smaller buildings and other facilities that lined the huge corridors inside of the complex. It made them think of a mall. The corridors were large enough for a cruise ship to pass through. There were lights running at the tops and bottoms of the corridors, along the walls. It was a very bright, clean, white light. The structures were made of some kind of metal. Keith's scientific mind wondered if it was earthly or an alien metal. There were aliens and humans scattered throughout the corridors, going about their business. All of the humans were in the white, radiation-type suits, but only a few of the aliens were. Nick noticed that the largest group walking together was a pair. He told his companions that they should split up and spread out. "Tracey, you come with me. Mandy, you and Keith find out and get whatever you can. I guess if anything goes wrong, just head back to the bay ... that is, if you can find it again." Nick said as he glanced around the huge complex. "What exactly are we looking for?" asked Mandy. Nick's heart sank. He didn't have a clue what he was doing. "Anything. Guys, we're just going to have to wing it." he said. "Good luck." said Mandy. "Same to you." Tracey said. The two groups headed in separate directions.

* * * * *

The preacher watched carefully as the young girl studied the controls of the alien aircraft. Amber was talking to herself and repeating what control did what. He was surprised at Amber's intellect for such a young age. *I bet if all of this stuff hadn't happened, she would probably have a very good career ahead of her.* Preacher Briggs thought. Amber felt as if she had a good grasp on how the aircraft operated. "You seem to be very adept at learning those controls, Ms. Kentwood." said the preacher. Amber turned and smiled back at Preacher John Briggs. "Thank you, Preacher." she said. He could sense her discomfort, but also felt her sincere effort to let him know that she didn't hate him. It made him feel a little better. As the preacher watched Amber, he began to memorize the controls that she was calling out. He felt like he could probably pilot the aircraft himself, also, if need be. *Maybe not as good as the young lady, but sufficiently.* he thought.

* * * * *

Mandy and Keith had entered many of the small buildings and doorways that lined the corridors. For the longest time, they were continually disappointed. There were alien clothes shops, food shops, gift shops ... it was indeed like an alien mall. They constantly apologized, wondering if they were supposed to enter particular shops or not. The biggest reactions they got were mildly irritated looks from the shop keepers. Finally, they struck gold. Mandy and Keith had found the armory.

There were two aliens behind a caged wall, as if they were in jail. The bars shone brightly, like chrome. Inside of the protective cage, behind the aliens, there was a large, door with bars, through which you could glimpse a variety of weaponry, including ones that were identical to what Mandy was carrying. Immediately, the alien on the left said "You're not supposed to be in this area." Keith looked at Mandy expectantly. She raised her eyebrows. Keith looked back at the alien that had spoken. "*Mohtaka.*" Keith said to the alien. He and Mandy began to approach the cage. The alien on the right began taking sidelong glances at the alien on the left. He slowly and inconspicuously began to shake his head, to warn Mandy and Keith that the other alien was not one of Kaletta's followers. "What's going on here?" the alien on the left said, with hostility. He began walking toward what appeared to be a communications panel on the wall, inside of the cage. Mandy understood. She drew her weapon and fired it at the alien, that was reaching for the communications panel. The alien slumped to the floor, unconscious. The other alien leapt back with surprise. Mandy already had the weapon trained on him. "*Mohtaka?*" Mandy asked more intensely. The alien nervously responded. "*Tohmondra.*" he said. "Good." said Mandy, nodding. "We need some kind of explosives." said Keith. "I can't do that. I've got to have authorization to open the armory door. Stun me with your weapon and leave quickly!" exclaimed the alien. "We've got to have those explosives!" Mandy shouted. "I'm already going to be in a lot of trouble, for getting taken by surprise. I'll help you any way I can, but I can't give you explosives. They'll kill me if they find out I'm a traitor!" said the alien as he began to panic. Mandy adjusted the weapon's setting. "I'll kill you, if you don't open that door and give us what we need." said Mandy. Keith looked at her to see if she was bluffing. He couldn't tell. Neither could the alien. "They know when this door is opened. Once it's opened, without authorization there will be a complex-wide alert sounded. You can't possibly get away." said the alien. "Okay, you're dead." said Mandy bluntly, as she straightened her arm out, extending the raised weapon toward the alien. "Wait! I'll open it!" he exclaimed. He let Keith and Mandy inside of the cage and keyed in a code on a keypad next to the large, door. Slowly, the door slid open. They all walked in. There were strange looking weapons on shelves overflowing inside of the large room. "Do you have any powerful explosives?" Keith asked. "These are the strongest we've got." said the alien, pointing to black, plastic-like cases of round, silver cylinders. "How do they work?" Mandy asked. "They're very simple to operate. They can be detonated by impact, or the top of the cylinder can be turned to set a time limit. Each click from a turn is roughly equivalent to one-half of your earth minute." said the alien. There were twelve cylinders to a case. Each cylinder was roughly the size of a round oatmeal box. They were very lightweight. Keith picked up one and looked at it closely. He could see the ring around the top, where it was to be turned. He pointed it out to Mandy. "Understand it?" he asked her. "Yep. Don't drop it and don't turn the top, unless you want it to blow something all to heck." she said. "Great." said Keith. Mandy returned her weapon to the inside of her suit. She and Keith each picked up a case of the explosives. Keith almost dropped his case, when an alarm began to sound. "Be careful with that! A few cases are enough to destroy us all!" exclaimed the alien. An alien voice began to speak softly, barely above the whine of the synthetic alarm sound, over the intercom system. Speakers were located throughout the complex. There are intruders inside of the complex. All personnel please report to your designated areas. Please follow procedural guidelines and protocol for this contingency. A soft, human female voice announced, following that of an alien's voice repeating the same message in their tongue. The large door to the armory began to slowly slide shut. "Come on!" said Keith, as he rushed through it. Mandy and the alien followed him.

* * * * *

Nick and Tracey were both amazed at what they saw. They had walked all the way to the other side of the grand complex. They were at the end of one of the huge corridors. There was an archway, in front of them with a sheet of bright, light, sparkling within its borders. Aliens were walking into the archway. They would sparkle, flicker, and then fade into a light silhouette. "You can still see them, but it's like they've lost some of their color." Tracey whispered to Nick. "I see that. Look, one is coming this way, out of the arch." he said. The faded alien on the other side of the arch sparkled and flickered. As he stepped out of the arch, his image became normal. "What is that thing? Is there a very restricted area beyond that arch? Is it some kind of weapon detector maybe?" Nick asked. Tracey shook her head. "It's not the same on the other side of the arch, though. It's like a huge room instead of a corridor. It doesn't look like the same construction. There's a lot more people over there, too." said Tracey. "You're right. What makes that side of the arch so special?" said Nick. He motioned for Tracey to follow him into one of the alien shops.

Nick's stomach rumbled, when they entered the shop. It was an alien bar and grill. He didn't know what kind of food they ate, but he knew it sure smelled good. He and Tracey approached the counter, where an alien was looking at a computer terminal, reading a strange, alien text. "*Mohtaka?*" Nick asked, with a goofy grin. The alien looked around to make sure no one could hear him and then said "*Tohmondra.*" The alien poured the two humans a beverage. Nick took a big gulp of his. "Not bad," he said. Tracey began to sip hers. "I've never tasted anything like it." she said. "What do you need?" the alien asked. "Information. What part of the complex is past the archway?" Nick asked. "The complex? That's not part of the complex. This complex is actually a large craft, designed to be submerged. The archway is a direct transport to the mother ship." said the alien. Tracey and Nick looked at each other with wide eyes. "The mother ship? What do you mean?" Tracey asked. "It's the craft that my people arrived in. Most of them are waiting on it." said the alien.

Nick hesitated before he spoke again, gathering his thoughts. "Let me get this straight. The archway leads to the spacecraft that you came on, and all of your people are on it?" Nick asked. "Yes. *Most* of my people are on it." repeated the alien. "The rest of them are in this complex, right?" Tracey asked. "This one ... and the others." said the alien. "Others? There are more complexes?" asked Nick. "Six more. One for each major continent of the Earth." said the alien. "There are seven complexes? Darn!" Nick exclaimed. The intruder alarm began to sound. "Oh,no!" Tracey exclaimed. Nick and Tracey rushed toward the door to the shop. "The archway won't be open very long, now. They begin shutdown procedures after the alarm has sounded!" the alien yelled after them.

* * * * *

The commotion the alarm had caused was extensive. Humans and aliens were running up and down the corridors, frantically trying to reach their designated areas. Mandy and Keith did not look out of place as they went as fast as they dared with the cases of explosives. The alien that was with them headed in the opposite direction. Shop keepers ran from their shops. Some, like Mandy and Keith, carried cases with them. Some of the aliens were snapping off orders to some of the humans. "You, there! Come here!" exclaimed an alien, that had just stepped out of his shop. He had been shouting to Mandy and Keith as they were hurrying by. Without stopping, Keith looked back and said "Bite it, lizard-face!" The alien looked stunned from the rebellious remark. Mandy looked over at Keith and smiled. He smiled back as he shrugged his shoulders. They continued their fast-paced gait.

* * * * *

Tracey and Nick ran through the crowds of aliens and humans, that were rapidly trying to get to their designated areas. Most of the aliens were heading through the bright, energy-field of the archway. After several minutes of running, they reached the aircraft bay.

* * * * *

"Look what we've got!" exclaimed Mandy as Nick and Tracey ran into the bay. Mandy and Keith had arrived at the bay a few minutes before Nick and Tracey. "What?" Nick asked as he and Tracey hurriedly approached. "These cylinders are explosives. There supposed to be very powerful!" exclaimed Keith. "We've got one of the cases loaded in the aircraft." said Mandy. "I hate to disappoint you, but we've got some awful news." said Nick. "What is it?" asked Mandy. "There are seven complexes in all." said Tracey. They described the archway and where it was to Keith and Mandy. "Oh, my." said Mandy, with an exhausted look on her face. Keith lowered his head and said "I guess we tried." Nick put his hand on his head as if he had a bad headache. "Tried my butt." he said, finally. "Everyone get into the aircraft. Wait five minutes, then leave the complex. After you're above it, drop the case on it." said Nick. Nobody moved. "Where do you think you're going?" Mandy asked Nick. "I'm going to the archway." he said. "Nick ..." Mandy began. "There's no time! This is our only chance!" he exclaimed. "I'm not going to let you!" exclaimed Mandy. "I love you, Mandy." said Nick. "Nick! You're not going!" Mandy exclaimed with fear. Nick drew his weapon and fired at Mandy on a stun setting. He quickly grabbed her and kept her from dropping to the floor.

* * * * *

"Please don't leave me tied up with all of this going on!" Preacher Briggs begged Amber. They could hear the group's conversation outside of the aircraft. "You know I can't untie you. You'll be okay." said Amber. "Please, I'm so scared. Do I look like I could hurt anyone to you, now?" he asked. Amber looked back at him and his pitiful, frightened expression. "At least, loosen them they're hurting me!" the preacher begged. Amber hesitated and then got up from the pilot's seat and walked back to where the Preacher was sitting. She reached for his hands, but he was already free. "Boo!" he said as he grabbed her, dragged her to the door and pushed her out of the aircraft. She screamed with fright as she held her hands out to break her fall. He closed the door to the aircraft. "How did he get loose?" Keith asked Amber, as he helped her up. "I don't know!" she yelled, with the anger directed at herself. The aircraft quietly rose up off of the bay floor. Although it wasn't a smooth motion, Preacher Briggs was indeed, able to maneuver the aircraft. "How does he know how to fly that thing?" asked Nick. "I guess he watched me practicing." said Amber, sullenly. The aircraft began to move forward toward the doors that led to the huge corridors of the complex. "What's he doing?" Keith yelled. The aircraft began to push and break through the large doors. "He's heading for the archway!" yelled Amber, letting her feminine intuition take over. "Everyone into another aircraft! Go, go, go!" yelled Nick. Metal fragments and rubble fell in some places where the sturdy aircraft had pushed its way through the bay doors. The preacher had maneuvered the ship out into the corridor. Tracey, Amber, and Keith carried Mandy's unconscious body into one of the other aircraft. Nick remained near the broken bay doors. Keith loaded the other case of explosives. "He doesn't know how to work the timers, Nick! You've got to turn the top of the cylinders, or cause an impact. One click of a turn is roughly equal to thirty seconds! How's he going to set them off, unless he just crashes into something?!?" exclaimed Keith, over the loud whine of the alarm. Nick yelled back to him "I don't know! Take off!" Amber came to the aircraft door. "Come on!" she yelled. "There's no time to argue! Do you want us *all* to get killed? Take off now, for crying out loud, and drop those explosives in five minutes!" Nick yelled. He turned and ran after the craft that the preacher was flying. They watched him until he was out of sight. "Let's go." said Keith, as he dashed back into the aircraft. "What about Nick?" Amber asked. "If we all die, he will have died in vain. You don't want that, do you?" Keith said. Amber didn't answer. They closed the door. Amber piloted the ship. They began to rise straight up, toward the ceiling. The ceiling opened up, and a voice rang out over the aircraft's intercom. "You're clear!" said Kaletta. She had been monitoring their activities in the bay. "Whew! I'm glad she came through for us!" exclaimed Amber. The aircraft rose up, out of the bay, and over the great lake.

* * * * *

Nick had to run fast. The craft piloted by Preacher Briggs, was moving very slowly, but much faster than Nick thought he could run. It was wobbling unsteadily, back and forth, from left to right. The preacher was definitely not a *good* pilot, but he was getting the job done. He was hovering only a few feet above the corridor floor. The humans and aliens that were already in a frenzied flight, began to hurry that much more, when they saw the oncoming, unstable aircraft approaching. Nick finally caught up to the aircraft. The sophisticated vehicle had no evident exhaust, which made it possible for Nick to clamber on top of it, knock on it, and try to get the preacher's attention. He had no luck. They approached the energy-field archway.

* * * * *

Amber had the aircraft hovering, several hundred feet above the open platform door of the alien complex. They waited. One minute passed. Amber looked toward the back of the vehicle, where Tracey was sitting beside Mandy, who was still unconscious. "How's she doing?" Amber asked. "Fine, I guess. She seems to be breathing normally." Tracey answered. Two minutes passed. Keith began to pace back and forth, while Amber stared at the video panel that displayed the platform several hundred feet below them. Mandy began to move around, and show signs of regaining consciousness. Three minutes passed. "Still no sign of Nick?" Tracey asked. "No." Amber and Keith responded at the same time. They were both staring at the video panel. Four minutes passed. Mandy opened her eyes. "Where am I?" she asked with fright, as she sat up. "We're safe. We're on one of those air vehicles, above the complex." Tracey answered. "Where's Nick?" Mandy asked quickly, as she began to remember what had happened. Everyone was quiet. "Where's Nick?" Mandy yelled. "He's still down there." said Keith. Mandy stood up and rushed to the front of the aircraft and watched the video panel with Amber and Keith.

Five minutes passed. There was still no sign of Nick. "What are we going to do?" Amber asked. "We're going to do what Nick said to do." said Keith. "What's that?" Mandy asked. "We're going to drop these explosives on the complex." said Keith. "But he's not out yet!" Mandy yelled as she began to get hysterical. "He may have already been captured ... or worse ..." said Keith, hesitant to mention death. "We've got to go back for him! Please, don't do it!" Mandy exclaimed, as she began to break down and cry. Keith went to her and hugged her. "We've got to." he whispered to her. With Mandy still in his embrace, he motioned for Tracey to open the door. She did. A cool breeze began to whisk around inside of the aircraft. "Get them ready." Said Keith to Tracey. Tracey pushed the case of explosives next to the open door, stopping at the edge. "Mandy, we have to do this or everything that Nick wanted to do was for nothing." Keith said. Mandy knew he was right, but she wasn't about to give affirmation to blowing up the only man she had ever really loved. Keith Nodded, and Tracey pushed the case out of the door way.

* * * * *

Nick felt light headed, but only briefly, as he passed through the energy-field that pulsed inside of the archway. The aircraft with Preacher Briggs inside, and Nick Tyler on top was instantaneously transported to the inside of colossal space vehicle located behind the planet Jupiter. The space vehicle was in a perfectly synchronous orbit with Jupiter, remaining behind it, out of Earth's detection, although, now, it no longer mattered.

The alien aircraft came to a stop, and gently came to rest on the floor of the large, open area inside of the colossal space vehicle. Nick jumped down from the aircraft and began to pound on the door. He was surprised when it opened a minute later. Nick walked in just as the Preacher sat back down in the middle of a circle he had made from the explosive cylinders. "You shouldn't have followed. There was no sense in you risking yourself, too." said the preacher. "I wasn't about to let anyone risk their life to do this. I was going to do it alone." said Nick. "You followed me because you didn't think I had the guts to do this, didn't you?" asked the preacher. "I wanted to make sure. I also needed to tell you how to detonate the explosives." said Nick. "Only a fool couldn't figure that out. All I had to do was turn the tops of them." said the preacher. Nick's eyes widened. His heart lurched in his chest. He felt sick to his stomach. "You turned them?" Nick asked in panic. "Yep." said Preacher Briggs. "When? How many times?" Nick asked hysterically. "Just now. I just finished the last one right before I let you in." said Preacher Briggs. "How many times!?" Nick asked frantically. "Well, there's twelve of these cylinders ..." the preacher began. Nick interrupted. "No! How many times did you turn each cylinder!?!" Nick exclaimed. "Five times," said the preacher. Nick felt dizzy. They had been talking for at least a minute. It had to have been at least a minute before the Preacher had opened the door. Depending on how close to half of a minute the alien timers were, there was no more than about thirty seconds left, before the first cylinder exploded. "Come on! We've got less than thirty seconds to get the heck out of here!" shouted Nick as he ran for the aircraft door. The preacher didn't move. "Come on!" Nick yelled. "I'm not going. This is my punishment for what I've done. Maybe He will truly forgive me." said the preacher. Nick didn't have time to argue. He ran out the door.

* * * * *

"Amber, go!" he exclaimed, as he hit the button and the door closed with a hiss. Keith, Mandy, and Tracey were all thrown to the floor from the aircraft's sudden burst of acceleration.

28

Heard 'Round the World

The blast was tremendous. A funnel of flame, smoke, water, and debris erupted from the platform, out of Lake Superior. As the debris began to splash and settle all around, there was another huge explosion. The platform flew to pieces, in all directions. Water, flames, and heavy materials traveled hundreds of feet into the air. There were ear splitting sounds of multiple explosions booming from the spewing funnel in the lake.

* * * * *

Simultaneously, there were six other explosions around the world. The other six complexes located on the remaining continents of the Earth were destroyed in a manner consistent with the Lake Superior explosion.

* * * * *

Amber slowed the aircraft to a complete stop, then hovered it down to the ground on Keweenaw Point. "Are you all okay?" Amber asked as the craft gently touched down on the paved surface of the road. Keith helped Mandy and Tracey up from the floor of the alien aircraft. "We're all okay." he said. "I'm so sorry about Nick." Amber said as she stood up. Mandy's face was expressionless. Her eyes were wet, from her tears, but she felt numb and empty inside. Amber went to embrace her, but Mandy would not let her. "I'm going to be sick. I need to go outside." said Mandy. Keith opened the door. He, Amber, and Tracey, all followed her out. Mandy held her stomach, bent over slightly, and began to retch. Amber stood beside her, with her hand on Mandy's back. "I love him so much." Mandy said, as she began to cry again. "I know you do." said Amber. "I hurt so bad!" Mandy exclaimed loudly and hoarsely. Amber hugged her tightly. She did not push her away this time. Tracey and Keith stood around them. Suddenly, there was a rush of air, and another alien aircraft set down next to the one Amber had piloted down. The other alien aircraft's door opened.

29

"Nick" of Time

"Sorry I'm late." said Nick as he stepped out of the alien aircraft. "Nick!" Mandy exclaimed, as she ran to him. She almost knocked him down she was running so fast. They embraced. "I love you, Nick Tyler!" Mandy said, through tears of joy. "And I love you, Mandy Richards." said Nick, as he gently swung her around in a small circle. "Very much." he whispered softly into her ear.

* * * * *

"How were you able to fly that aircraft?" Amber asked, after Nick and Mandy finished their embrace. "I didn't." said Nick. "She did." he added. Kaletta stepped out of the alien aircraft. "We are very thankful." said Keith. Kaletta was silent. "Yes, thank you very much." said Amber. Kaletta shook her head slowly, from side to side and placed her hand on her brow. "What's wrong?" Mandy asked. Kaletta lowered her hand back down to her side. "My people killed nearly all of your people. You four are some of the few humans left alive on your planet, and you're standing there, sincerely thanking me for my help. You humans are a remarkable race. I'm sorry for what my people have done." said Kaletta, as she drew her weapon and pointed it at herself. "Kaletta, don't!" exclaimed Nick, as he jumped toward her, and grabbed her arm. Kaletta fired the weapon, narrowly missing her own head. Nick wrestled the weapon from her with ease. She was probably stronger than him, but she wasn't putting up much of a fight. To the groups surprise, she began sobbing. "What's wrong, Kaletta?" Mandy asked, as she approached. There was silence. Finally, Nick spoke. "She betrayed her people to do what was right and help us. She is probably the last of her race." he said. After a few moments of silence, Keith finally asked "What happened back there? Kaletta was the one who opened the upper platform doors for us. We saw the platform explode. How did y'all get out?" Nick motioned for everyone to sit down. Kaletta sat with them, but she was quiet and withdrawn.

* * * * *

"When I finally caught up to the aircraft the preacher had left with, I was able to climb up on top of it. I couldn't get the preacher to open the door. He hovered it right through the archway, and then stopped." said Nick. "So you were on the mothership, right?" asked Mandy. "Right. Just as the alien had told Tracey and I." said Nick. "Preacher Briggs opened the door I guess within about a minute after he had stopped. When I went in, I saw that he had placed the explosive cylinders in a circle, and had sat down right in the middle of them." said Nick. "What personality was he exhibiting?" asked Keith. "I really don't know. I think it was somewhat more of a normal one, but definitely not completely normal. He said that his sacrifice would be his punishment for his other misdeeds. He said that maybe God would truly forgive him, if he made this sacrifice." Nick explained. "Were the timers set on the cylinders?" asked Mandy. "Yes, they were! He said that he had turned them five times! I knew at least about a minute had passed before he opened the door. We had talked for about a minute. That left about thirty seconds for me to get out of the mothership!" exclaimed Nick. "How did he know how to set the timers?" Amber asked. "He just figured it out. I assume he didn't have any idea of how much time each click was for. He said he just turned them five times each." said Nick. Everyone was silent. "So, how in the world did you get out of there?" exclaimed Keith with excitement. "I tried to get the preacher to leave, but he wouldn't budge. There was no time to try and coax him. I had to go. I ran from the aircraft. I knew there was no way I was going to be able to make it back to the bay. Even if I did, I knew those explosives would be coming down before I could get there. I just began to run away from the archway, deeper into the mothership." said Nick. "I bet you were really scared." said Mandy. "I sure was. And you were all I could think about, Mandy. I wasn't as much scared of dying as I was scared of not seeing you again. I didn't know if you were safe, either." Nick said. Tears had formed in his eyes. "I was scared too, Nick." said Mandy. Nick and Mandy squeezed each other's hands. Keith and Amber did as well. Nick placed a hand on Kaletta's shoulder, and Mandy hugged Tracey. They both managed to force small smiles to acknowledge the effort and concern. Nick sensed that they were waiting for him to continue his account of the events on the mothership. He did so. "After I had started running, an aircraft quickly hovered up beside me, and stopped. At first, I thought it was Preacher Briggs. I thought that maybe he had come to his senses. The door opened, and it was Kaletta." I rushed in and told her that we only had a seconds before the explosives went off. She turned the aircraft around, and then I warned her of the explosives you were supposed to drop. Kaletta was remarkably calm. If she was as scared as I was, then she certainly didn't show it." said Nick. Everyone looked at Kaletta. "I was scared." she said. Nick shifted positions where he sat, and then continued. "She turned the aircraft around *again*, and headed back down, deeper into the mothership, the same direction I had been running. We zoomed right through another archway located several hundred feet from the one the preacher and I had entered. The corridor we entered looked identical to the one back at the Keeweenaw Point complex, but I knew it wasn't. When we got to the bay doors, Kaletta fired a weapon from the aircraft, and blew a hole in the corridor wall, where the doors were, exposing the bay. We went through the hole and headed toward the ceiling. She keyed in a code on the aircraft's computer terminal, and the upper platform door opened. We had barely cleared the platform door, when the mothership exploded." said Nick. "Where did you come out?" asked Keith. "At a complex located off of the coast of Venezuela. It was our base for your South American continent." said Kaletta. "The mothership and two complexes were destroyed?" Mandy asked. "Yes. Actually, all of the complexes were destroyed." said Nick. "How were they ALL destroyed?" Amber asked. Nick looked at Kaletta. "The blast from the mothership erupted through the seven archways, before the archways themselves were actually destroyed, sending enough destructive force to wipe out all of the complexes and some of the surrounding areas as well." said Kaletta. "Wow!" said Amber. "But we don't know for sure, right?" asked Mandy. "Do we ever know anything for sure?" asked Nick. Mandy held Nick's chin and turned his head toward her and looked into his eyes. "I know for sure that I love you." she said. "And I know that I love you," said Nick. "See? I knew *that* too." said Mandy with a smile.

Epilogue

Two alien aircraft were all that were left from their ordeal. Kaletta, with Amber assisting, taught Nick, Mandy, and Keith how to pilot them. For no particular reason, they flew them to where the Little Tennessee River flowed through the Great Smoky Mountains. They found an area along the river that had been untouched by mankind or alienkind. They installed a generator in the river for power. They built some houses. They built some storage buildings. Together, over the years, they built a small community. They could have rebuilt an existing town...but this town was truly theirs. There were no animosities between the humans and Kaletta. There was much loss on both sides. They all remembered their losses with some sadness, but were now concentrating on what they did have and were looking to the future. Kaletta did more than her part assisting in the creation of this new town. The humans welcomed her input and advice. She had some technology which she shared, and an alien viewpoint that was unique. She was glad to be made a part of the new world. After all, this was now her new home, too. Mandy's child was the first born into their new world. The night she was born, Nick saw a deer walking through their vegetable garden. It was one of many more animals that began to reappear after the devastation. During their trips out to other areas of the world, they found other humans that had survived, scattered around. Most of them could not recall what had happened to them during the cataclysm. The disappearance and reappearance of some of the animals and those humans would always be a mystery. The crickets chirped loudly, the night of their child's birth. Mandy and Nick gave their new little girl the name *Hope*.

"Gather up the fragments that remain, that nothing be lost." - St John 6:12.

Author's Note

I hope you enjoyed the story! I was a very young man when I wrote the original. I made a few minor changes, most of them grammatical and punctuation corrections. I also removed profanity from this version. I'm not a moralist, but I do believe that there is a time and place for everything. I do not believe the removal of expletives diminishes this story at all. Maybe you *still* found some errors. If you did, hopefully it did not detract from your experience. When I was reviewing my original files, I found one dated as early as 1997. That's 25 years ago as of the date of this second publishing - 2022! As I edited the story, I found it absolutely amazing that I did not give a cell phone to any of the characters, and no one had even used a landline. From my research, I found that the first mobile phone was available around 1983, and the first smartphone was available around 1994, so they were definitely around then. Although I appreciate and enjoy my smartphone and all of the amazing things it can do, there's another example of things that we don't always need in a story or to live and enjoy life!

Take care,
Chad Gunter

Other Books by the Author

THROUGH THE HAND GLASS

When a police detective is injured during an investigation, the department declares him unfit to continue performing his regular field duties. Afraid of the direction his new career path may take, he chooses to leave the department and start his own business as a private investigator. Shortly after establishing his new vocation, a chain of hapless events necessitates him to include his son, who has Down syndrome, in the operations of his new business. After multiple quandaries, he soon discovers that his son is much more capable than he could have ever imagined. However, there are times when a private investigator's work can be very dangerous.

PULLING ON THE STRINGS

A scientific team led by two physicists have been contracted by the government to work on a project focusing on the development of a revolutionary, new transportation technology. They have made an astounding breakthrough by establishing proof of the string theories that are necessary for the technology to function. However, when an arrogant, government official takes control of the project, his conceited and haphazard methods cause dramatic and dangerous changes to the world as we know it.

PROJECT NEMESIS

Alan and Cord are two average-bodied gym rats that find a flyer posted at their local gym with an advertisement for a clinical trial that focuses on fitness. With the hopes of gaining some muscle mass and increasing their physical performance, they decide to join the trial. Shortly after they begin the program, they are discretely warned by one of the host facility's janitors to quit and never come back. After a little snooping and some frightening discoveries are made, they quickly decide to leave the study and blow the whistle on their findings. However, the powers behind this unsanctioned and illegal government testing program have no intention of letting the men destroy their potential profits and interfere with their nefarious schemes. As the design criteria of Project Nemesis - Nano-technologically Engineered Muscularly Enhanced Surgical Implantation System - begins to reach apotheosis, everyone involved gets way more than they bargained for!